CHERRY AMES, ISLAND NURSE

The CHERRY AMES *Stories*

Cherry Ames, Student Nurse
Cherry Ames, Senior Nurse
Cherry Ames, Army Nurse
Cherry Ames, Chief Nurse
Cherry Ames, Flight Nurse
Cherry Ames, Veterans' Nurse
Cherry Ames,
Private Duty Nurse
Cherry Ames, Visiting Nurse
Cherry Ames, Cruise Nurse
Cherry Ames at Spencer
Cherry Ames,
Night Supervisor
Cherry Ames,
Mountaineer Nurse
Cherry Ames, Clinic Nurse

Cherry Ames,
Dude Ranch Nurse
Cherry Ames,
Rest Home Nurse
Cherry Ames,
Country Doctor's Nurse
Cherry Ames,
Boarding School Nurse
Cherry Ames,
Department Store Nurse
Cherry Ames, Camp Nurse
Cherry Ames
at Hilton Hospital
Cherry Ames, Island Nurse
Cherry Ames, Rural Nurse
Cherry Ames, Staff Nurse

☆   ☆   ☆

The VICKI BARR *Flight Stewardess Series*

Silver Wings for Vicki
Vicki Finds the Answer
The Hidden Valley Mystery
The Secret of Magnolia
Manor
The Clue of the Broken
Blossom
Behind the White Veil
The Mystery at Hartwood
House
Peril Over the Airport

The Mystery of the
Vanishing Lady
The Search for the
Missing Twin
The Ghost at the
Waterfall
The Clue of the
Gold Coin
The Silver Ring Mystery
The Clue of the
Carved Ruby

The Mystery of Flight 908

"Here's a loose one!" Tammie cried out

CHERRY AMES
ISLAND NURSE

By

HELEN WELLS

~~~~~~

NEW YORK

GROSSET & DUNLAP

Publishers

Contents

CHAPTER I

A Call from Dr. Fortune

CHERRY STOPPED IN FRONT OF HILTON HOSPITAL and glanced at her wrist watch. She was not due to be on duty for twenty minutes. She stood for a moment, enjoying the sunshine and the fresh, sweet air of spring. What a glorious morning!

In the sky overhead a small plane was circling about. Shading her eyes with her hand, Cherry watched it descend slowly in widening spirals and bank to come in for a landing at the new private airfield outside Hilton.

"I wouldn't mind being up in a plane myself this morning," Cherry thought dreamily.

"Nurse Ames, you have a very bad case of spring fever," she heard a voice boom.

Startled, she turned her head and saw Dr. Watson, a wide grin on his face, beside her. "Check that fever at the door," he told her, laughing. "It's highly contagious."

"Good morning, Doctor. You sneaked up or I would have heard you," she accused him as he started up the walk. Her eyes followed his clumsy, bearlike figure to the entrance. She had a warm spot in her heart for Dr. Ray Watson who was in charge of Men's Orthopedic Ward. He had been patient, understanding, and always cheerful when she was a nurse on his ward.

Cherry was now one of the Emergency nurses and was often the nurse on one of his cases. Dr. Watson handled accident cases involving orthopedics, such as fractures and other conditions which caused interference with the use of bones and joints.

Cherry forgot the sunny sky and the plane and walked through the door into the antiseptic smell of the hospital. The quick change from the air outside made her nose prickle as always, but the odor quickly became familiar and she felt completely at home.

"Good morning, Miss Ames."

"Good morning, Mrs. Peters," Cherry returned the greeting from the head nurse on Orthopedic Ward.

"Whenever you've had enough of Emergency," Mrs. Peters said with a smile, "remember, I can always use an extra nurse."

"I'll say we can," declared Nurse Ruth Dale, as she came in the door and fell in step with Cherry. "We're always short of nurses, you know that."

"Hospitals are always short of nurses," agreed Cherry. They went on down the corridor toward the section where the nurses had their lockers. "It's a complaint as common as the common cold, or haven't you heard?" Cherry asked airily.

Ruth made a face at her, taking the teasing in good nature. She and Cherry had been on duty in the same ward and had been good friends for a long time. Ruth was frank to say that Cherry was shining proof that beauty and brains went together. Cherry's dark-brown, almost black eyes, black curly hair, and red cheeks, which had won her the name of Cherry, always called forth admiring remarks. Her patients appreciated her cheerful presence.

The doctors and head nurses recognized Cherry's ability and skill as a nurse and her deep interest in nursing. She could use her head when clear thinking was needed. And she was as good as a detective about getting at the facts of anything.

On her part, Cherry never seemed to be aware that she was special and that is what endeared her to her fellow nurses.

She and Ruth reached the lockers and put their handbags, and the light sweaters they had worn around their shoulders, in their lockers. As they adjusted their caps, Ruth said, "You know, Cherry, I miss you. I guess we all do."

"Why, Ruth, what a sweet thing to say!" exclaimed Cherry. "But why be so sad?" She grinned at her friend. "I may not be on the same ward but I'm right in the same hospital, so we just might arrange to lunch together sometime."

"What a creature!" cried Ruth. "Taking my kind words and turning them into a feeble joke." She peered over her shoulder to see if her petticoat showed below her uniform. "But, Cherry, honestly I envy you sometimes. No, I don't think envy is the right word. Admire is better. You are always, it seems, on interesting cases. That last case you had . . . Tom . . . Dick . . . oh, that young man with amnesia."

"Oh, you mean Richard Albee," Cherry said. "Yes, I'd never been on a psychiatric case before, and working with Dr. Hope was a wonderful education for me in a new field. Before that, the mind always seemed to me to be rather a separate thing. But now I realize just how interrelated mind and body are—how the mind can actually affect physical well-being." Cherry hung her head in mock chagrin. "Sorry, Ruth," she apologized, "my mind must be back in nurses' training at Spencer School. I really didn't intend to give an early-morning lecture."

"Now, I know what your next job is going to be," Ruth announced solemnly. "You're going to be a lecturer on psychosomatic diseases, or in simple plain English, those diseases which can be traced to emotional disturbances." She smoothed down her uniform. "Well, I'm off to the bones-and-joints department. See you later." Ruth went bouncing off.

Cherry turned down the corridor leading to Emergency. Here interns were on duty round-the-clock. In addition, there were a head nurse and assistant nurses and doctors quickly available on call. Medical help had to be on hand day and night to take care of any casualty that came in.

An ambulance with a driver was always ready to answer an emergency call.

In Emergency the staff was on the move all the time. Seldom more than an hour or two passed without a call. It sometimes seemed to Cherry that for as small a city as Hilton, Illinois, there was an unusual number of people who were just plain accident prone.

Walking along the corridor, all the familiar sounds of the hospital greeted Cherry's ears: the whisper-like tread of feet, glass gently clinking, nurses speaking low or crisp, a child crying or laughing, the complaining voice of a patient. Over the intercom came repeated calls for one of the doctors to call the chief resident physician's office.

Before Cherry reached the door of the Emergency room, she heard the motor of the ambulance start up outside and saw one of the young doctors come hurrying down the hall, clutching his bag in one hand and buttoning his white jacket with the other.

"You'd think people would give a man time to get dressed," he complained, "before they started getting sick or burned or smashed up or something."

"Where are you off to?" Cherry asked.

"That new private airfield," replied the doctor and dashed out to the ambulance, which took off at once.

Trouble at an airfield usually meant only one thing—a crash of some sort, with people broken or burned or both. Cherry recalled the plane she had seen in the air only minutes ago. How sad if something had happened to it or anyone in it.

Emergency at Hilton Hospital consisted of a large room and three cubicles for patients. It was near the wide doors for receiving stretcher cases. A head nurse and assistant nurses were on duty there at all times. Cherry was one of the nurses on duty from eight A.M. to four P.M.

Cherry was just entering Emergency when she heard her name called. Dr. Phipps, one of the assistant resident physicians, came striding through the Emergency entrance, carrying a sturdy-legged boy across his outstretched arms. The boy's face was streaked with blood and he was unconscious. Two boys in T shirts and blue jeans, their faces almost as white as the patient's where it was not coated with blood, trod upon the doctor's heels.

"Is Chuck hurt bad, Doc? Chuck isn't going to die, is he, Doc?" the boys kept repeating like a refrain.

"Of course not. Of course not," Dr. Phipps told them. With a nod, he directed Cherry to one of the cubicles and she helped him lay the youngster carefully on the narrow bed.

Chuck's two jean-clad friends would have barged on in, but Cherry captured them and got them seated, assuring them in a clear, confident voice that their friend was going to be all right. "Dr. Phipps will take good care of Chuck," she said. "The doctor let you come in with him because he knew you wouldn't make a fuss. Now, you just wait right here quietly."

They obeyed her, sitting straight in their chairs and staring out of big, round eyes, rather like two owls.

Cherry returned to the cubicle. While she cleaned the blood from the boy's face, the doctor continued to examine him. Then she fixed cold packs which Dr. Phipps applied to the bruised and swollen, but unbroken nose.

Upon regaining consciousness, Chuck was frightened. Cherry soothed him and in a few minutes he began to touch the pack on his nose softly with his finger, his freckled face crinkling up as he sort of grinned around the pack.

"Guess I broke it," he said tentatively.

"No. Lucky you," said Dr. Phipps. "But a fine way to start spring training for the baseball season is all I can say."

"My brother Charlie had the same thing happen to him when he was a kid," Cherry said. "Stood right in the way of a bat and got clipped."

"That's right, how did you know?" asked Chuck. "But it wasn't Mickey's fault. You see, Johnny was pitching, Mickey was batting, and I was catching . . ."

"And you stood closer to the batter than a catcher ought to," interrupted the doctor. "Result: you were knocked unconscious and got a bloody nose. You don't have to tell me—I was passing in my car and I saw the whole thing. How did you think you got here so quickly?" he asked with mock gruffness.

"Does my mother know?" Chuck asked.

Dr. Phipps nodded. "One of the ballplayers raced off to tell her."

Within a few minutes, Chuck's mother arrived.

"His nose is swollen. Don't be alarmed if it bleeds a bit more," Dr. Phipps told her. "Take him home and keep an ice bag on it."

"Thank you, Doctor," she said. "And on my way home with Chuck, I will drop these two members of Hilton's all-star ball team at school," she added, nodding at the two boys, who, relieved to find their friend's injury was not serious, went whooping out to the car.

Cherry saw Chuck and his mother out into the hall. "Don't be surprised," she warned, "if Chuck has a real beaut of a black eye." She went back inside.

"We don't have enough business," the head nurse commented dryly to Cherry, as Dr. Phipps was preparing to leave, "so some of our doctors have to find patients and bring them in on their way to the hospital."

"Hospital, rats!" exclaimed Dr. Phipps inelegantly. "I did it solely in the interest of Little League baseball."

The telephone rang and the head nurse picked up the receiver. She listened a moment, then handed the phone to Cherry. "It's for you. Dr. Joseph Fortune calling. Very important."

Dr. Fortune—Dr. Joe to all in Hilton Hospital and the city of Hilton as well—what in the world could he want? Cherry wondered as she took the receiver.

"That you, Cherry? Well, thank heaven!" Dr. Fortune exclaimed as soon as Cherry spoke. "Now, I want you to get over to the Private Wing and get everything ready in Suite 6 for an emergency patient."

"But, Dr. Joe," she protested, "I'm on duty here in Emergency."

"I know. I'll arrange it with the head nurse," said Dr. Fortune. "I'm calling from the airfield, the private one outside town. Man had an ulcer attack, a bad one. I've done what I could and we're bringing him to Hilton immediately. Now, here's what I want you to do," and Dr. Joe gave her a list of instructions. Then he asked to speak with the head nurse.

"Of course. Of course, it's all right, Dr. Joe," she was saying as she waved Cherry out the door.

Cherry walked briskly through the hospital to the Private Wing. It was a special wing of the hospital where patients, who could well afford to pay for comfort, service, and beautiful surroundings, might spend the time during their illnesses.

Dr. Fortune's patient must be wealthy, Cherry thought. It made her happy to think that Dr. Joe, whom she had known all her life, would for once be well paid. So often he was not very well paid and more often than that he gave his service freely to those who were sick and unable to pay him at all. Dear Dr. Joe with his seamed, sensitive face and boyish spring to his step.

Inside Suite 6, Cherry paused a moment to look around. She was not familiar with the rooms. They were tastefully decorated and furnished. There was nothing to remind the patient that he was in a hospital. In fact, he might well imagine himself in a fine hotel. Cherry caught a glimpse of herself in a mirror in the sitting room of the suite. Her practical, antiseptic uniform certainly struck an odd note.

CHAPTER II

The Three from the Plane

WITHIN A VERY SHORT TIME, CHERRY HAD THE BED-room of the suite ready for the patient and everything prepared according to Dr. Joe's instructions. But just to be sure, she stood for a moment in the middle of the room to check again.

Near the head of the bed were the two intravenous stands—"I Vee" stands the nurses called them—which a hospital attendant had brought from the supply room where such equipment was kept for use as required. From one stand hung the pint container of normal saline for the administration of saline, an injection into the veins of a salty solution, which would have to be given the patient. The other stand would hold the bottle of blood plasma for the transfusion, after the patient's blood had been typed.

"The man had a sudden hemorrhage and lost a lot of blood," Dr. Fortune had told Cherry over the phone. "He'll need a transfusion."

She also had ready oxygen tank and mask, ther-

10

mometer, cotton swabs, adhesive tape, bottles of anti-septic and anesthetic, sterile gauze pads, needles and rubber tubing used in giving intravenous treatment, hypodermic needles, and other medical supplies.

Everything had been done that could be done beforehand. The bedroom had become a little hospital within a hospital. Cherry gave a nod of satisfaction and looked at her watch. The ambulance should be back from the airfield at any minute.

She had already alerted the laboratory to have someone ready to make a blood test. Now, she heard a knock and a voice call "Miss Ames," and Millie Reynolds, one of the laboratory technicians, came bustling in.

"They have *all* arrived. I saw them bring in the patient, so I didn't have to wait for your call," she announced. Millie was a blond, blue-eyed girl who looked as if she could not possibly have a brain in her head, but she was one of the best laboratory technicians at Hilton.

Cherry had noticed the accent on "all" and she smiled. "How many exactly, Millie, are there with the patient?" she asked. "You make it sound as if he were royalty accompanied by his entourage."

"Well, it's practically that," Millie said. "I heard this big, handsome hunk of man say something about his uncle, Sir Something-or-other, that's the patient. . . . Imagine a patient with a title! Isn't it exciting?"

Millie did not have time to tell about "the others" with the sick man, for there were sounds of movement in the hall and a hospital attendant rolled in a still form. He was followed by Dr. Fortune and two young men, one of them in pilot's uniform, his visored hat in his hand.

Dr. Joe gave Cherry one of his warm smiles, then glanced at Millie.

"Doctor, Miss Reynolds is ready to check the blood at once," Cherry explained.

"Very good." Turning to the two young men, Dr. Joe told them, "You may wait here in the sitting room."

The patient was taken into the bedroom and the door closed. Things must be done quickly. There was no time to waste; a man's life was threatened. In the next instant, the three of them—Dr. Joe, Millie, and Cherry—became an efficient team.

The man was unconscious. His flesh was gray and clammy from loss of blood and shock. His pulse was rapid.

The mask was placed over his face and the flow of oxygen regulated.

The rubber bands and tubing for the injection of saline were adjusted. Cherry wiped a spot over the veins of one arm with a swab of cotton soaked in antiseptic. The doctor injected a small amount of a local anesthetic to numb the arm slightly, then deftly pushed the hollow needle into a vein in the bend of the patient's elbow, and the slow drip of salty liquid into the vein began.

Meanwhile, Millie had quickly pricked a finger and drawn a little of the man's blood into a tiny vial. Off she went with it to the laboratory, where she would test it immediately for blood type. The transfusion could not be given until this was known.

Aided by Cherry, Dr. Joe proceeded with the examination of his patient.

At the airfield and during the ride in the ambulance, the nephew and the pilot had told the doctor what had happened. And between listening through his stethoscope, checking of pulse and breathing, gently feeling the patient's stomach and abdomen, Dr. Joe gave Cherry bits and pieces of information.

"Fellow collapsed in a plane not far from here. . . . Name's Barclay—Sir Ian Barclay. . . . Haven't seen him in ten years. . . . Owns iron mines up in Canada. . . . Peptic-ulcer case. . . . Nephew said doctor up there had been treating him for some time. . . . Lloyd Barclay, that's the nephew's name, said his uncle was getting along pretty well . . . then this sudden hemorrhage. . . . Uncle went to make telephone call to check on how things were going in his mines. . . . Found there was trouble. . . . Sudden anxiety probably set off this attack."

The door opened. Dr. Joe's and Cherry's heads turned as one to Millie, with a bottle from the hospital's blood bank in her hands.

"Group O, Rhesus positive," she told them, "and the patient's is the same—perfect match." She walked briskly over with it, then as briskly out again.

Group O was a common blood type and could be safely given to anyone belonging to the other main groups—A, B, or Ab—just as long as the Rhesus factor was the same. That Sir Ian Barclay's belonged to this common type was certainly a bit of good luck right at the start, Cherry thought, as she swabbed his arm with a bit of antiseptic-soaked cotton in preparation for the transfusion.

Cherry and Dr. Joe could only wait now while the science of medicine, which had taken man many centuries to develop, took over. Sir Ian's body must be supplied with oxygen, so he breathed it into his lungs through the snoutlike device invented for the purpose. The salt and liquid his body had lost were being replaced by the saline. And life-giving plasma flowed into his veins from the bottle hanging from the stand.

Sir Ian Barclay was breathing easily now. Some of the grayness had given way to the faint violet of returning blood. The flesh was warmer and drier.

Familiar as she was with the care and healing of the sick, Cherry never ceased to wonder at the miracle of medicine. And one was taking place before her eyes right now.

It was true that there were failures, and there was so very much yet unknown about health and sickness —yet what science and the doctor could do was no less a miracle. Perhaps that was why it was the most important thing in the world to her to be a nurse, Cherry thought. She was a part of the wonder of healing.

That was the way Dr. Joe had always felt too. He had given his whole life to medicine. A small, friendly man who spoke slowly and haltingly— who would think of him as a hero? He was a modern-day hero, nevertheless.

She saw Dr. Joe put his hand on Sir Ian's forehead. Then he listened again to the patient's heartbeat.

"Looks as if we'll bring him through," Dr. Joe said, straightening up.

He pulled up a chair beside the bed and nodded to one near Cherry. "Might as well sit as stand at this point," he said.

They sat in silence. Cherry knew that Dr. Joe would add nothing to what he had told her before. That much information he had given her because she needed to be oriented to the case. Sir Ian Barclay at the moment was not a personality to the doctor, but a sick human being who must be made well again.

As Cherry sat beside Sir Ian, the lean, powerful figure, with its strong, bony face and gray-streaked black hair, began to pique her curiosity. "Here is a man," she thought, "who looks as if he had great strength of character. He is a wealthy mine owner. A Canadian with a title. He is on a tour of mines in the United States. He calls home, hears bad news, collapses shortly afterward."

"Sudden hemorrhage of a peptic ulcer," Dr. Joe had said. People with ulcers had sudden flare-ups—that Cherry knew. Bad news could cause an attack. What had been the nature of the bad news that had caused this wealthy man, with the sturdy look of an eagle, to collapse, she wondered.

A mumbling came suddenly from the bed.

Both Cherry and Dr. Joe jumped.

Sir Ian Barclay had opened his gray eyes and was staring at them.

Dr. Joe removed the oxygen mask. When the man tried to raise his head, the doctor bent over and put a gentle hand on his shoulder.

"Don't worry, Sir Ian, you're coming along all right," he said. "Just take it easy now."

Sir Ian lay back quietly. His eyes searched the doctor's face for a moment, then he spoke slowly, but Cherry caught the odd lilt to his voice and a Scottish twist to his words.

"I'd recognize you anywhere," Sir Ian said. "You've not changed in ten years, Dr. Joseph Fortune." He made an attempt at a smile.

The way he spoke immediately enchanted Cherry. Later—but that was after she had come to know the sounds so well—she always thought of the lilt of a Scottish tongue as a kind of spoken music.

"Now, Doctor, you can't keep me here," Sir Ian was saying worriedly. "It's most important. I must go home."

"Now, now," Dr. Joe soothed him. "You are not to worry about anything. Nothing is important at all but getting well." It took a bit before Dr. Joe's confident manner calmed him. He kept insisting that Dr. Joe tell him exactly when he could go home, which, of course, the doctor could not tell because he could not know.

Finally, Sir Ian dozed off, murmuring, "I shouldn't have left Jock to manage alone . . . too much for him. I must get back and straighten things out."

CHAPTER III

Sir Ian Barclay

AFTER THAT FIRST DAY, SIR IAN'S "WHEN CAN I GO home?" was to ring daily in Cherry's ears. At first it was pleading and sounded strange, coming from a man six feet tall. A man who had ruled thirty years over the island of Balfour, off the coast of Newfoundland, and the famous Balfour Iron Mines, as though he were a king.

But the plea in his voice was because he was physically weak. The moment he began to get better, his usual commanding tone returned and he demanded to know rather than asked. And he tried to bully Dr. Joe into releasing him, and failing that, he tried playing on Cherry's sympathies.

She always answered primly, "Dr. Joe will tell you when he thinks you're well enough to make the trip to Balfour Island."

Sir Ian would first glare at her, then smile ruefully. "Remind me of my Meg—warmhearted, strongheaded, and high-spirited," he would say.

17

And he would talk to Cherry about his daughter Meg, who was twenty and the apple of his eye. She was abroad, visiting relatives in Scotland and England.

And he forbid anyone to write Meg about his illness and "ruin her holiday." He had set his mind on getting well.

"Take it easy," Dr. Joe kept cautioning him. "To worry or fret is the worst thing you can do. Forget about business." Then, with a grin, he would add, "Enjoy ill health and get a good rest for three or four weeks."

Sir Ian had followed the doctor's orders to the letter. In return for his obedience, however, he expected to see such great improvement every twenty-four hours that he would be told he could return to Balfour Island.

Lloyd Barclay and the pilot, Jerry Ives, were as much in the dark as Cherry and Dr. Joe as to exactly why Sir Ian was insistent upon returning home. They all knew by now that Sir Ian's news over the telephone concerned closing a mine.

"But that's no reason for Uncle Ian to go home," Lloyd said. "Number 2 mine, which has not been worked for years, was reopened shortly before we left. When Uncle Ian called our Mine Office, he learned that the walls of one tunnel were too weak for the miners' safety. Mining had been stopped until the walls could be reinforced. A thing like that can happen when an unworked mine is reopened. Of course Uncle Ian was terribly upset to have it happen so soon after starting out on a long tour. But he's

"When can I go home?" Sir Ian asked Cherry daily

building a mountain out of a molehill, if he thinks he must go back to see to things."

"People who worry sometimes build mountains out of molehills," Dr. Joe pointed out. "Your uncle told me that he had not been away from Balfour for any length of time in many years. Obviously he feels, whether it is true or not, that without him there to run the mines, they won't run properly."

"But he seemed to be fine when we started on the tour," Lloyd said. "He even joked with Jock Cameron about coming back to find himself out of a job. Mr. Cameron has been superintendent of Balfour Mines for over thirty years. Uncle Ian left Jock Cameron in charge while he was away."

"I remember Sir Ian joking with Mr. Cameron just before we took off in the plane," agreed Jerry Ives. "Sir Ian was in good spirits."

"But then later on," Lloyd said thoughtfully, "Uncle Ian seemed—well, detached, I suppose you'd call it. It was as though something worried him and he was trying not to let it bother him. For instance, he would sit lost in thought. I would have to repeat a question a couple of times before he heard me. Then he would rouse himself, so to speak, and answer. Once in a while we might even talk for a time. But it was not until we made our first stop at some iron mines in the upper peninsula of Michigan that he became enthusiastic about anything. There he saw some methods being used in the mines which he wanted to try out in our Balfour Mines. He was as excited as a boy over the idea."

"But later in the plane," Jerry added, "Sir Ian

began to brood again. It was not until he had seen the mines here in Illinois that he was in fine fettle. You remember, Lloyd, your uncle remarked what a lot he got out of seeing how efficiently mines could be operated. Then, of course, he made that telephone call to Balfour Island."

"When the three of us got into the plane and took off," Lloyd said, "I noticed Uncle was, as Jerry called it, brooding again. When he told me the bad news, I tried to cheer him up, but with no success. In a little while, he was in pain and—well, we all know the rest."

They were all four—Cherry, Dr. Joe, Lloyd Barclay, and Jerry Ives—in the sitting room of the suite. It was almost a week since Sir Ian had been admitted to Hilton Hospital, but it was the first time they had talked informally. Lloyd had visited his uncle as often as he was allowed. The pilot had come at least once a day, but they had both been under too much strain to want to chat. Today Sir Ian was definitely showing improvement and they all felt somewhat relaxed.

Perhaps it would be fairer to say that Jerry Ives was trying to give the appearance of being at ease.

"I wonder what he's so nervous about?" Cherry thought, as she watched him shifting from side to side and drumming his fingers on the chair arm. "Probably has a date with one of the nurses and is trying to think of a graceful exit line."

He had a pleasant, engaging manner that was very attractive and went well with his red hair and impudent grin. He had met some of the girls and dated a couple for dinner and the movies. He had taken one date for a ride in the private plane and given her the thrill of her life. They thought the Canadian pilot was "wonderful."

Midge, Dr. Joe's daughter, who was a junior volunteer nurse's aide at Hilton Hospital, came in as usual after school one afternoon. Jerry was just leaving the hospital, "looking so absolutely marvelous, it took my breath away," Midge told the Ames family with whom she was having dinner that same night. "And he said 'hallo' in that marvelous English accent."

Charlie, Cherry's twin brother, gave a most ungentlemanly snort. "A fellow says hello and you are swept off your feet," he commented. "You surprise me, Midge. You really do. I thought you were beginning to grow up and be sensible."

Charlie and Midge would have wound up in a good-natured but noisy discussion of Jerry Ives, if Mrs. Ames had not switched the conversation to Lloyd Barclay.

Cherry, in talking about Lloyd Barclay, had to admit that the nurses did not think he was "wonderful."

"I should say not," Midge piped up. "He never has more than two words to say to anyone: 'Good morning,' 'Good afternoon,' 'Good evening.' The nurses think he's just a snob. Even Millie Reynolds, who, when she first saw him thought he was a real dreamboat, decided he's too standoffish for her." Midge shrugged and added, "Of course, he does have the most beautiful manners."

Cherry had thought Lloyd was a little snobbish too at the beginning, but having seen him every day, she knew better. He was a kind, warm person, but very sensitive and shy. "The nurses ought to see him now," Cherry thought, as she, Dr. Joe, Jerry Ives, and Lloyd sat talking in Sir Ian's sitting room. "They would get a very different impression."

His manner was alive and his voice friendly as he talked with Dr. Joe about the hazards and diseases of miners.

"My uncle will never forget how you saved Mr. Cameron's life that time you were up in Canada," Lloyd said suddenly when they came to a pause.

"And don't think I will forget it, either," declared Dr. Joe. Turning to Cherry, he explained in a hurt tone, "Cost me several sleepless nights and almost cost me my fishing trip." Then he went on to relate how he was on his way to meet some friends in Canada to go fishing. His plane had run into fog, got off course, and had to come down at St. John's, Newfoundland. At the same time, a little mail plane from Balfour Island landed with Sir Ian and a man dying of pneumonia.

"Always carry my case with me," said the doctor, "and it came in handy that night. Managed to keep the old man—he must have been very near eighty—alive until we could get him to the hospital. The fog was so thick, it was a wonder that the ambulance could get from the hospital and back again."

"That old man you saved," Lloyd said, "died years later. Lived to the ripe old age of ninety-five. He was Jock Cameron's father; the Camerons have been superintendents of our mines ever since there were any Barclays on the island. Uncle Ian always remembered how you pulled old John through and stayed with him until he was out of danger. And he has kept up with your work, Dr. Fortune. Every time your name is mentioned in the news—maybe you've read a paper before some medical society—Uncle Ian always takes note of it. As a matter of fact, just before he collapsed, he asked Jerry the name of the nearest town. Jerry told him Hilton and that it had a private landing field. Then Uncle told Jerry to land and me to call Dr. Joseph Fortune."

Jerry Ives had begun to fidget with his hat, then asked abruptly, "Doctor, now frankly, it's going to be some time before Sir Ian will be out of here, isn't it?" Seeing the puzzled look on Dr. Joe's face, he hastened to explain, "Well, you see, there's no need for me to wait around to fly him back. At least that's what I told Mr. Broderick. And he said for me to get back to Montreal right away."

Cherry saw Lloyd Barclay's face flush with quick anger.

"Jerry, I told you I would call Mr. Broderick at the end of the week," Lloyd said acidly. "By then I hoped we'd have a clear idea of just what my uncle's condition was. Besides, I just might want to continue the tour of mines alone. So by what right . . ."

"I don't know what your uncle may have told you, Lloyd, but Mr. James Broderick's my boss. He gives the orders so far as I am concerned," Ives said, shrugging.

"If Mr. Broderick wants you back in Montreal, then you'd better go," said Lloyd.

As Ives rose, he glanced rather sheepishly at Cherry and Dr. Joe. "I don't want you to feel I am running out on Sir Ian," he apologized, flashing them a boyish grin, "but as I told Mr. Broderick when I called him, there doesn't seem to be much point in my hanging around here, so . . ." His voice trailed off.

"I'm sure there's none," Dr. Fortune said, getting up. "Now, if you'll excuse me, I'll go have a look at my patient." He nodded to the pilot and left.

"I have a bag to pack," Jerry said, "so I'd better get going." He started across the room, then stopped and turned around. "Say good-by to Sir Ian for me. Hope he gets well soon, I honestly do."

"Thank you, Jerry. I'll tell him," Lloyd said, and getting up followed the other to the door.

"Good-by, Miss Ames," called Jerry, and the next moment he was gone.

Cherry felt embarrassed at having witnessed the scene between the two, in spite of the fact that as a nurse she was certainly exposed to many intimate family affairs. Lloyd Barclay would probably feel that she was in the way, so . . .

"Please excuse me, Mr. Barclay," she said. "It's time for your uncle's feeding." And she hurried out of the room.

Dr. Fortune was pulling the sheet up, after having examined Sir Ian once again. "You're coming along. You say no pain to speak of, that's good," Dr. Joe was remarking. "We'll take some X rays, and then we'll see what we'll see. I've been in touch, as you know, with your Dr. Douglas Mackenzie on the island and he's given me a summary of your case. Sounds like a fine young physician. Ulcer of the duodenum, that first inch of bowel next to the outlet of the stomach, he told me. A small crater there, no perforation." The doctor looked around to Cherry. "Ah, there you are, Miss Ames. I was on the point of calling you." Nodding toward Sir Ian, he went on, "The patient wondered if you'd mind very much writing a letter and mailing it for him."

"Why, of course not," Cherry said cheerfully. "I'll just prepare Sir Ian's four-o'clock feeding . . ." She caught the glint in the mine owner's eye and stopped. "Correction, milk with cream in it. Sir Ian finds the word 'feeding' distasteful," she told Dr. Joe.

"Call it nectar and ambrosia, Miss Ames, if that will help," suggested the doctor solemnly.

"Even nectar and ambrosia become a bit monotonous," declared Sir Ian, "if given at intervals of every two hours. What name did you give this treatment, Doctor? Oh, yes, I recall—Sippy. And it is quite aptly named, if I may say so."

Dr. Joe laughed. "It happens, Sir Ian, that that was the name of the doctor who devised the treatment of peptic ulcer—Dr. Bertram Sippy of Chicago."

"I refuse to believe it," said Sir Ian. "It is too pat altogether."

Cherry had prepared the mixture of equal parts of milk and cream for the feedings throughout the day and had stored them in the suite's refrigerator. She had only to pour out the correct amount in a glass and hand it to Sir Ian with a glass tube to suck through.

Dr. Joe picked up his bag. "I'll look in on you in the morning," he told Sir Ian. "The last test showed the acid in your stomach is being kept down at night, so I won't come poking and dosing. You can get an uninterrupted night's sleep."

Both Cherry and Sir Ian watched the doctor's slight figure move with quick boyish step across the room and out the door.

"There is a *doctor!*" announced Sir Ian.

"And a fine man," Cherry added. She went over to the writing table in the bedroom and sat down. Getting out note paper and an envelope from the drawer, and her pen from her pocket, she said, "I'm ready for that letter now."

Sir Ian sucked noisily for a moment, then dictated:

"Dear Jock: Here I am in hospital. You'll see the name and address at the top of the page. Attack of ulcers. Nothing to worry about. You know I've had upsets before this. I am writing to let you know that I have decided not to continue the tour of mines in the United States and Mexico. As soon as I am well enough to travel, I am returning to Balfour.

"No doubt Mike McGuire has told you I talked with him when I called the Mine Office. Now, I am not blaming you, Jock, for what happened in Number 2 mine. Don't think for a moment that I am. But with the reopening of Number 2 and the opening of the new mine, as soon as the preliminary work is done, anything is liable to happen. I should not have let James Broderick persuade me against my better judgment to take the tour at this time.

"I did discover some important new developments in operation during visits to two mines here in the States, so the time has not all been wasted."

There was a pause, then Sir Ian continued, "Here's the name and address where you send it: Mr. Jock Cameron, Piper's Cove, Balfour Island, Newfoundland, Canada."

Cherry addressed the envelope and held the letter while Sir Ian signed it with a flourish.

"Thank you, Nurse. You'll find some airmail stamps on the desk, I believe," he said.

She found them, licked one, and placed it on the letter.

"Now, I suppose you're going off duty," Sir Ian complained pettishly. "It's past four by your watch, I see. And you're going to leave me to the tender mercies of that starched tyrant."

"Mrs. Hendrickson is very capable and kind," Cherry defended the nurse on duty from four P.M. to twelve midnight.

At that moment Mrs. Hendrickson came in, big and bustling and efficient, and took over.

"See you at eight sharp in the morning, Sir Ian," Cherry called out from the doorway.

"Don't forget to mail my letter."

"I won't," she promised.

On going into the sitting room, she was surprised to see Lloyd Barclay still there.

"Why, Mr. Barclay, I thought . . ." she began.

"Thought I'd gone?" he asked. "No, I waited to ask you if you'd stop and have an ice-cream soda with me. The doctor passed through a bit ago and he asked me if I was waiting to see my uncle. It was too bad, he said, but no more visitors were allowed. 'Who wants to see the auld rascal?' I asked. 'I am waiting to see that bonnie lass of a nurse, Miss Ames. I am going to ask her . . .' "

Cherry shook her head sadly and then crinkled her eyes at him. ". . . her to have an ice-cream soda," she finished for him.

"And what did the doctor say?" demanded Lloyd, and answered himself in the next breath. "He said it was a brilliant plan."

"You, Mr. Barclay," Cherry accused him, "are simply a younger Barclay than the one in there," pointing to the other room. "You look like him, talk almost like him, and you are a wheedler, and I suspect a bully just like him."

Lloyd Barclay's dark-gray eyes regarded her sadly. "I dinna haud with compliments and ye canna take ma mind off its purpose with fancy words," he said righteously. "How about that soda?"

"I accept with pleasure, Mr. Barclay," she said in her most ladylike tones.

CHAPTER IV

Lloyd

~~~~~~

CHERRY FELT GAY AND AT EASE WITH THE WORLD
when she went to her locker to get her handbag and
powder her nose, after telling Lloyd Barclay to meet
her in the visitors' lounge.

She had reason to be happy. Her patient was mend-
ing. And didn't she have a date with a man most of the
girls would have given their eye teeth to go out with
in spite of their feeling that he was "snobbish."

Lloyd saw her in the doorway of the lounge, got up
quickly, and came forward. He observed Cherry
admiringly, then said shyly, "I'm surely a lucky
fellow to be taking out such a pretty girl."

"Thank you, sir," she told him demurely.

They went outside. "I'm depending on you to lead
us to the best soda in town," he warned as they
started down the walk.

"If you're like my twin brother Charlie, it's the
place where they give you the two biggest scoops of
ice cream," she informed him.

30

"Any brother of yours is bound to have the right idea," he assured her.

He wanted to know about Charlie, so Cherry launched into an enthusiastic account of her brother's work. At the corner, she stopped to drop Sir Ian's letter in the mailbox and went on talking. "Charlie was always, even as a kid, interested in aeronautics," she told Lloyd. She giggled suddenly. "You should have seen that room of his! It was piled to the ceiling with models of planes."

Walking down the street, from almost everyone they passed, it was "Hi, Cherry!" or "Hello, Miss Ames!" and an interested glance at the handsome stranger at Cherry's side.

"People in this town all seem to know you," remarked Lloyd.

"I've lived here all my life and my parents before me, so I suppose the Ames family could be called old-timers. That accounts for it," explained Cherry.

"That's the way with us on the island," he said. "Everyone knows the Barclays. Most of us on the island are what you call old-timers. Our families came there in 1750 and a good many have clung to the rocky place like lichens ever since. In fact, until my uncle's generation, none of the Barclays left the island except to go to school in Scotland or for travel in Europe to round out their education. But I rather spoiled the tradition by going to the Colorado School of Mines and working in the States."

Hilton's favorite ice-cream parlor was charming and old-fashioned. Cherry and Lloyd sat talking over their strawberry ice-cream (two huge scoops) sodas.

It was Lloyd really who did the most talking and Cherry listened. He seemed to feel the need to talk to someone.

As he said, "In the past week my uncle and I have become better acquainted with you than people we've known for years. We've come to think of you as not only a nurse, but as a friend, too. It may seem strange to you, but Uncle Ian and I are shy. It's often hard for us to make friends. He covers up his shyness by being stiff and arrogant, while I give the impression of being sort of a cold fish. At least, that is what the fellows told me at the Colorado School of Mines until they really got to know me." He paused, then continued, "But with you, Cherry—I hope you don't mind my calling you Cherry, and you call me Lloyd —with you it's different, somehow."

For a time, he went on talking of the island, the various families, his student days at the mining school. Suddenly, Cherry, who busied herself with her soda, caught a more serious tone in his voice. She sensed that he was leading up to a confidence of some sort.

"Cherry," he began at last, "I suppose you're wondering about Mr. Broderick, Jerry Ives, the plane, and all the rest."

"It isn't any of my business, Lloyd," Cherry pointed out gently and smiled. "But, frankly, now that you yourself brought it up, I *am* curious."

"I was hoping you would be," he returned with a grin. "Especially since I hope that we can be good friends."

"Carry on then, Friend Lloyd," Cherry encouraged him, keeping her tone light so that he would not feel shy or embarrassed.

"Let's begin, then, with Mr. James Broderick," said Lloyd. "He is a man of wide interests in shipping, construction, plastics, mines, mining machinery, and equipment. Now, Uncle Ian had to have all new machinery and equipment to start work on and then operate the new mine, the Number 10 you've heard us speak of.

"Uncle Ian went to James Broderick and arranged to purchase what he needed for the mine through companies that Broderick controlled. Uncle Ian had to borrow a very great deal of money to do this."

Cherry shook her head. "Oh, dear, to owe money worries everyone. Of course Sir Ian is worried."

"Don't look so sad," Lloyd told her. "To borrow money in business and industry, Cherry, is an everyday matter. It isn't the borrowing of itself that makes a business safe or unsafe. It's how *much* can be borrowed with safety by a particular company.

"Balfour Mines is a family-owned company. Uncle Ian, my cousin Meg, Aunt Phyllis and Uncle George in England, and I—we own the mines. There are few such companies that have survived. And for a very good reason. It takes too much money to run them and compete with enormous industrial and business concerns—the giants. You know yourself, Cherry, that the small grocery store finds it hard to compete with chain stores and supermarkets.

"It's the same with the Barclay-owned iron mines. We are little compared with the modern giants. When Uncle got the money for the new Number 10 mine, he had to borrow *more* than was safe for our family-owned mines. He stretched his credit too far. He has been able so far to make payments on the loans. But he hasn't been able to meet the full payments regularly. And Broderick would leap at the chance to gobble up Balfour Mines. I gathered all this from the few bits of information that Uncle Ian let drop when we were visiting the mines."

Cherry frowned, trying to understand how it all fitted together.

"You seem puzzled," Lloyd said.

"I am," Cherry replied. "I don't understand Mr. James Broderick. He's a hardheaded businessman, ready to gobble up the Barclay mines one moment, and the next, he's sending you and your uncle on a mining tour in his private plane with his personal pilot, Jerry Ives."

Lloyd burst into a hearty laugh. Cherry's face must have changed its expression to a wounded one, for he apologized, "Cherry lass, don't look so hurt. It's just that James Broderick is so easy to understand. He's simply interested in taking over companies that are not going as well as they should and making them operate efficiently and profitably. In the process, Mr. Broderick becomes tremendously wealthy and powerful. He advanced money for machinery and equipment for Balfour Mines, so he's interested in seeing that the mines are operating at top level if he ever has to take them over. If observing modern efficiency methods in other mines would help Uncle and me to do this, Mr. Broderick was going to see that we got to visit the most modern mines."

"Well, then," argued Cherry, "isn't Mr. Broderick taking a big chance? If you operate the mines very profitably, the loans will be paid off and Mr. Broderick can't gobble up the mines."

"But that's a chance he's willing to take," Lloyd said. "You see, either way he doesn't *really* lose. As for the Barclays, they have just about everything to lose if the loans can't be paid off."

"No wonder Sir Ian is so worried about the mines," Cherry mused aloud. "No wonder he was so upset over the trouble in that Number 2 mine you are re-opening." She thought of the letter Sir Ian had written Jock Cameron. Now she could understand why Sir Ian felt it urgent to return as soon as possible. He had to be there to see that there was no trouble in the mines. His being there would probably make no difference one way or another, but he *felt* he should be there. Trouble meant loss of money. He dare not let the mines lose money.

Lloyd turned his attention to his soda and took a last noisy suck. He gave Cherry a smile, as bright as the sun breaking through clouds. "Away dull care!" he cried softly in a bantering voice. "Ah, Cherry lass, 'tis a good thing there's na more to drink or there's na tellin' but I waud ha' tawked your ears off your bonnie head." He leaned back and considered her with mock seriousness. "Mind ye, I'm not one to throw my money away on a mere snippet of a gurl, but waud ye have another strawberry soda?" he asked.

Cherry thanked him, laughing at his imitation of a canny Scotsman, but told him she had promised to be home by five o'clock.

"I really must fly," she said, glancing at the time. "The Women's Camp Committee is meeting at our house tonight on final plans on day camps for children this summer. I'm supposed to help Mother."

Lloyd paid the check, then insisted upon taking her home in a taxi. "Will you have dinner with me one evening?" he asked as he left her at her door.

"Perhaps you'll come for dinner and meet my family," she countered.

"I would be delighted," he said. He ran down the steps and drove off in the cab.

"Who was that nice-looking young man who brought you home?" her father asked. He was sitting near the window in the living room, reading the evening paper.

"Yes, I think he's rather nice," agreed Cherry, stopping to preen herself before the hall mirror. She stuck her dainty nose in the air and announced in stilted accents, "He's only the nephew of the famous Sir Ian Barclay."

Mrs. Ames came in from the kitchen just then. Her sweet face was puzzled for a moment, then she smiled, her eyes twinkling in amusement. "Miss Ames, I don't like to interrupt an actress who is throwing herself into her part—and I do mean throwing—but . . ."

"I'll be right with you," Cherry sang out. She tossed a kiss to her mother and dashed upstairs to her room.

When dinner was eaten and the dishes washed, Cherry and her father escaped to the back porch and sat on the steps, leaving Mrs. Ames and the ladies to carry on their committee work inside the house. To escape the hectic preparations for the meeting, Charlie had decided to dine out that night.

"I'm to stand by in case they have any questions on health, physical examinations, and the like," Cherry told her father. Because of her experience as a camp nurse, she served as a sort of volunteer consultant to her mother's committee. Cherry gave one of her delightful little giggles. "Otherwise," she said, "the ladies prefer to do their own planning with no interference from fresh young things like me. I think, this year, they are going to hold the free day camp in the woods near the lake and take the children there and back each day by bus. Right now, they are in a swivet over how to raise some more money."

Mr. Ames groaned. "I smell a White Elephant Sale or a Spring Auction coming up. And your mother is going to make me give up one of my treasured possessions."

Cherry sniffed. "Something like that hideous desk lamp you bought because you felt sorry for the man? Or the stuffed owl that molted? You bought that, I believe, because you wanted to help the Boys' Taxidermy Club get started. If it weren't for the ladies' sales and auctions," she scolded fondly, "this house would soon look like a whatnot museum."

"Women!" snorted her father. "No appreciation of the finer things in life."

Silence fell on the two. They looked out on the lawn where trees cast mottled shadows in the moonlight. From Mrs. Ames's garden the odor of spring flowers was wafted to them by a little breeze which came up suddenly and as suddenly died away. There was a feeling in the air of contentment.

"Why don't you ask that young fellow to dinner sometime?" asked Mr. Ames apropos of nothing at all.

Cherry knew "that young fellow" meant Lloyd. "I already have," she said. "I know you and mother will like him." She talked about Lloyd and his uncle then for a while.

Her father listened, asking a question now and then.

"You know, Cherry," he said finally, "I think this whole ulcer trouble is probably due to worry over money. Sir Ian is sick with worry. That's an old-fashioned expression, but it is very apt at times."

"Yes, money worry is probably the clue to the whole thing," Cherry agreed musingly.

Without their being aware of it, the house had become silent and snatches of conversation no longer drifted out to them.

They heard a movement behind them and Mrs. Ames walked out on the porch. "Meeting's over and they have all gone home," she announced, then without a break continued, "Cherry Ames, I distinctly heard you use the word 'clue.' Now, you're not going to start playing Miss Sherlock Holmes again, are you? You'll end up in a book just the way he did," warned her mother, laughing.

"The Barclays are very interesting people," remarked Mr. Ames in a hurt tone. "And we were talking about them. I don't know how the word 'clue' came into the discussion, do you, Cherry?"

"I suppose it sneaked in when nobody was looking," replied Cherry, joining her father in teasing her mother.

"Oh, you two!" exclaimed Mrs. Ames. "Incidentally, while you were doing so much talking about the Barclays, did you decide to ask the young man to dinner?"

"We did," Cherry and her father declared in unison.

Cherry and her mother and father set a date which seemed best for everyone—Friday of the following week. The next day, Cherry was giving Sir Ian his noontime milk and cream when Lloyd came to visit his uncle, and she invited Lloyd to dinner. He accepted enthusiastically.

"The nerve of the chit!" exclaimed Sir Ian. "Asks you to a good dinner at the same time she's conniving with the doctor to keep me on Dr. Sippy's slops for three weeks."

Sir Ian might growl, but all the same, Cherry could see that he was enormously pleased.

"And what do I have to do to receive an invitation?" he demanded.

"Get well, sir," she told him cheerfully.

That was Saturday. It had been arranged for Cherry to have a day off on Sunday. It would be Monday morning at eight before she would be on duty again. By then, Sir Ian had already seen the disturbing news item in the paper, which changed everything.

~~~~~~

CHAPTER V

Meg

MONDAY MORNING, MISS PAGE, THE TWELVE-MID-
night-to-eight A.M. nurse, came out of Sir Ian's room,
looking worried and exhausted.

Cherry hurried up to her. "How is he?" she asked.
Sir Ian had been walking about a bit when she had
left him on Saturday.

"Things aren't going too badly now," Miss Page
answered.

Cherry cried, "You mean Sir Ian's worse?"

"Well, he had a relapse after I came on at midnight," Miss Page explained. "He was in great pain
and I had to call Dr. Fortune."

"What in the world happened?" demanded
Cherry.

The other shook her head. "I haven't the slightest
notion, Miss Ames. He was asleep when I relieved
Mrs. Hendrickson. She said he'd seemed all right.
He had sat up and even read the newspaper earlier in
the evening."

"How is the patient now?" Cherry asked.

"As I said, not doing too badly," Miss Page replied. "Dr. Fortune is in there with him."

Cherry opened the door and walked quickly into the room.

Dr. Joe was sitting at the desk, making some notes. He looked up as Cherry came in and stood beside him, after she had briefly observed Sir Ian's quiet form.

"Good morning, Cherry," Dr. Joe greeted her wearily. In a quiet voice so as not to be overheard by the patient, he continued, "We've had a setback, I'm afraid. It's a good thing you are going to be with Sir Ian. He has become extremely dependent on you. His attitude toward Miss Page and Mrs. Hendrickson isn't at all cooperative."

Dr. Joe sighed and returned to his notes. Cherry went over to the bed. Sir Ian lay quietly on his back, his gray-streaked black head turned to the side, his nose beaklike against the pillow.

"Looks just like a great sleeping eagle," Cherry thought.

All of a sudden, she was aware of one gray eye regarding her. "I've made rather a mess of things, Cherry," he said with a wan attempt at a smile. "All your good work for nothing."

"There, now," she told him, "don't fret. It's going to be all right. You don't hurt anywhere now, do you?"

"No, not for the moment," he answered.

Dr. Joe began to gather up his notes preparatory to leaving. "I'm going to call Dr. Mackenzie at Balfour Island and confer with him," he explained to Cherry. "Sir Ian was nauseated by the cream in the milk. He hasn't been before, as you know. Miss Page gave him plain milk, but he vomited that and suffered intense pain. There were no indications of hemorrhaging. I worked to get the acid in his stomach neutralized. He was in distress for some time, though, in spite of various treatments. That has been relieved, but I want him to go back on the Sippy regimen that we used at the beginning, that is, the hourly feedings instead of every two hours.

"If there is any hint that the cream may make him nauseous, don't mix it with the milk. Simply give him three ounces of milk.

"I know you realize," Dr. Joe said, as they walked through the sitting room, "how important mental rest is for people with psychosomatic diseases, such as ulcers. From the description Lloyd has given me of his uncle, I gather Sir Ian has always been an intensely hard-driving, hard-working man, who has been under unusually severe strain for a number of years. Acute anxiety brought on the attack in the plane, for Dr. Mackenzie told me when I talked with him before, that any major difficulty at the mines used to bring on mild attacks. Never anything so serious before. But I can't think of any nervous upset which might account for this relapse, can you?"

"No, Dr. Joe, I can't offhand." She stopped, then said quickly, "Unless Sir Ian was upset by Jerry Ives's leaving as he did."

"Sir Ian doesn't know yet that Ives has gone," Dr. Joe continued. "He didn't hear what went on Friday in the sitting room. And I asked Lloyd to say nothing about it. I mean, there was no point." Dr. Joe took a deep breath. "Do everything you can to put his mind at ease."

"Of course," Cherry promised. "Are you going to allow Lloyd to see him?"

"Yes. Not too long at a time. Sir Ian's very fond of his nephew. Might be upsetting if we kept Lloyd away just now," replied Dr. Joe. With that he left, saying he would be in again later.

Cherry moved about the room quietly, putting things in order, checking supplies, keeping a watchful eye on her patient. At nine o'clock she gave him three ounces of milk. The cream bothered him, he said, so she omitted it. He dropped off into a light doze.

She noticed that the wastepaper basket beside the desk was full. It had been overlooked, no doubt, when the room had last been tidied. But what made her decide to take it out and exchange it for the empty one in the sitting room, she could not guess. Or why she looked into it, she did not know. But she did. The greater part of the contents was a newspaper, neatly folded and tucked in at the side.

Cherry stood in the sitting room, about to set the basket down, when she found herself thinking back to what Miss Page had said, that Sir Ian had read the newspaper. What newspaper?

With a glance over her shoulder at Sir Ian to see that he was still dozing, Cherry closed the bedroom door and snatched the paper out of the basket.

Toronto Star stretched across the masthead in bold, black type. "Why of course," she thought. She knew Lloyd had arranged for his uncle to receive the *To-*

ronto Star by airmail special delivery at the hospital. She felt a prickle of excitement. Sir Ian must have read a news story or an item that disturbed him.

Holding the paper in outstretched arms, she began running her eyes up and down the columns.

At last her search was rewarded.

"Explosion in Mine" headed the one-column report. She raced on:

"Balfour Is., Nfld. Apr. 10. An explosion took place yesterday (that was Saturday, Cherry thought, counting backward quickly) in one of the mines here. No one was injured, according to a statement by M. F. McGuire, Assistant Superintendent of Balfour Mines. He could not account for the explosion. Operation of the mine has been temporarily halted for necessary repairs."

There was no question now in Cherry's mind about it. That short paragraph was the cause of Sir Ian's upset.

There was something in the story itself that struck Cherry immediately as wrong. Why was McGuire, the assistant superintendent of Balfour Mines, quoted? The person who should give out statements to the press was the superintendent in charge, Jock Cameron. Why had not Mr. Cameron done so?

She folded the paper back at the paragraph, ready to show Dr. Joe and Lloyd. Cherry looked about for a hiding place. Beneath the seat cushion of one of the chairs was as good as any. She slid it under and returned to Sir Ian's room.

Lloyd arrived a little after eleven o'clock, to find his uncle just finishing his milk. He carried a huge bunch of daffodils in one of those white molded-pulp vases which florists provide.

"Good morning, Cherry! Good morning, Uncle Ian!" he greeted them cheerily. "You're looking better, sir. That milk is doing wonders for your complexion; you are going to have a skin like a wee bonnie bairn's before long."

"And the wee strength of one," his uncle growled weakly.

"I brought you some flowers," Lloyd said, stating the obvious.

"Ay, but such a wee bunch," remarked Sir Ian. "Of course the color is bright and showy," he added grudgingly.

Cherry and Lloyd exchanged a knowing glance. They could see that he was pleased.

Lloyd placed the flowers on a table near the window where Sir Ian could see them.

Cherry said, "I'll leave the two of you alone awhile," and started out.

"There's no need for you to go, Cherry," Sir Ian told her. "I'm not in a talking mood today. I'd rather listen and I'd enjoy your company. So you and Lloyd sit down and talk," he ordered.

Cherry laughed. "Usually people tell me to sit down and *stop* talking," she said.

"Uncle Ian usually tells me the same thing," Lloyd remarked, "so this will be a welcome change." He drew up a couple of chairs and they settled into an easy conversation of small talk. Cherry knew that Lloyd was a good talker. Now she found that he was equally good at telling a story. He related a wonderful folk tale about an old Balfour Islander who became a pirate and returned to haunt the place.

"You see, Cherry," commented Sir Ian, "Lloyd's a true Barclay, knows all the old tales, loves the island. And he is going to make the best mining engineer Balfour ever had. No doubt he's told you he was graduated with top honors from the Colorado School of Mines. And he could have been a top man in the mining company where he worked. But he loves Balfour and he's there to stay."

Lloyd flushed at his uncle's praise and mumbled, "Thought *you* were going to listen, not talk."

"No, Sir Ian," Cherry said, "I had no idea how important he was."

"Just like him," Sir Ian agreed flatly. "Of course I approve of a certain degree of modesty. But my nephew overdoes it," went on Sir Ian as though Lloyd were not present. "Furthermore, he's overflowing with all kinds of ideas. Wonderful ideas, but highly impractical."

Sir Ian stole a glance at his nephew to see what effect his words had on him. Lloyd pretended not to notice, but he frowned with quick anger.

"It's my turn now to talk," Cherry announced abruptly. "Did I ever tell you about the time I was a nurse for a country doctor and got all mixed up in a campaign for mayor?"

Both men looked at her in surprise.

"You ran for mayor?" asked Sir Ian.

"You would have had my vote," declared Lloyd stoutly.

"And mine," echoed Sir Ian with equal conviction.

"You are both deliberately twisting my words," Cherry said, laughing. "I wasn't running for mayor, a man was."

This struck them both as funny. "Oh, a man! Fancy that!" they cried.

She had set them off and they were bent on teasing her. She not only did not mind, but she gave herself a mental pat on the back for getting the conversation back in the right key.

Lloyd's visit had lasted perhaps half an hour when he got up, saying that he had better run along. Between visits to his uncle, he had been spending time touring the area about Hilton to take a look at the various factories and industries, and some of the engineering projects. Cherry rose casually and followed him to the door.

"Wait out here," she whispered quickly. "I must see you." Then, for Sir Ian's benefit, she said loudly, "Good-by for now," and closed the door.

Sir Ian smiled up at Cherry as she returned and stood at the foot of his bed. "I don't know when I've had a more pleasant time," he told her. "I have a feeling you're what the Indians call 'good medicine.' I resent nurses on general principles. They boss me and I don't like being bossed."

Cherry grinned. "I boss you, too, but I try not to let you catch on," she pointed out.

"Ay, you're canny. You know just how to handle me to keep me from getting my back up," he said. "Few people are able to do that. Two only I can think of offhand—you and Meg." A little sigh escaped him. "I wish my Meg were here so she could meet you and get to be friends." His words trailed off. He closed his eyes.

Cherry waited, and when he did not open them, she went quietly into the other room.

Lloyd had been walking up and down slowly, lost in thought. He whirled to face her. Before he could ask any questions, Cherry darted to the chair, plucked out the newspaper, and handed it to him. "Oh, it's the *Star*," he said. "It must have been delivered to Uncle Ian after I left him last evening."

"Read that." Cherry pointed to the paragraph on the explosion.

Lloyd read it swiftly. "There must be something terribly wrong at Balfour!" Lloyd exclaimed, his voice low but harsh, his face angry. "This man McGuire— who does he think he is? If anyone gives a statement to the press it should be Jock Cameron; he's the superintendent."

"Could Mr. Cameron have been away when it happened?" suggested Cherry. "Perhaps he was sick."

"Oh, no, there's more to it than that," declared Lloyd. "Why, that red-faced bully! If that McGuire thinks he's going to usurp Cameron's place . . ." he broke off. "I'm going to find out what's going on up there. I'm going to Balfour!" He strode to the door. "Thanks, Cherry. You're strictly wonderful. Please give me a rain check on that dinner Friday."

With that, he was out in the hall. Cherry ran and called after him, "Where are you going?"

"Going to see Dr. Joe," Lloyd called back. "Tell him what I'm going to do."

By the time Dr. Joe came that afternoon to visit Sir
Ian, Lloyd Barclay had packed and was well on his
way to Balfour Island. He had called the nearest
airfield and chartered a plane.

"No one could stop him. He was determined to
go," Dr. Joe told Cherry. "And even if I could have
stopped him, I don't know whether I would have
been doing right. This is Lloyd's chance to show his
uncle that he is not a fool when it comes to managing
the affairs of the mines. And since his uncle is in no
condition to manage anything right now, let the boy
see what he can do. After all, he inherited his father's
shares in the Balfour Mines and he has a right to
look after his interests, to put it bluntly."

"His uncle doesn't think Lloyd's a fool," Cherry
said. "He's crazy about his nephew, I can see that."

"I know. I know," agreed Dr. Joe. "Of course he is.
But Sir Ian has no confidence in Lloyd's business
ability. He thinks the boy is a remarkable engineer,
but lacks administrative ability. He forgets that he's
never given Lloyd a chance."

"How are we going to break the news to Sir Ian?"
Cherry asked, sighing deeply.

Dr. Joe gave her what he might have thought was a
sly glance, but it was about as sly as a small brown
bear's.

"Sir Ian is going to have a very happy surprise.
Oh, I tell you, that boy, Lloyd Barclay, got the bit in
his teeth this morning and there was no holding him.
He called Meg Barclay in London. And she'll be
here as fast as jet planes and other modern convey-
ances of travel can fetch her."

To Cherry the time until Sir Ian's daughter arrived on Wednesday seemed to be endless. Luckily, Sir Ian assumed that his nephew was off taking a look around the country, which he had said he might do. So Cherry simply said nothing.

Sir Ian's condition showed some improvement, but he seemed depressed and moody. Cherry could rally him, but he was withdrawn and taciturn with Miss Page and Mrs. Hendrickson.

Then Wednesday came at last. And with it lovely Meg Barclay. She did not announce her arrival. She simply appeared in the doorway like a princess out of a fairy tale.

Sir Ian saw her and his whole face lighted up. She ran over to him and threw her arms about him.

"Oh, Da!" she cried, using the Scottish word for Dad. "Why didn't you tell me? I would have come sooner and taken you home."

"There, there." Sir Ian patted her dark head. "Don't take on now. I wanted you to have a good time."

Meg lifted her head and brushed away the tears that had gathered in her eyes. She was all sunshine again. "But, Da, after the first two weeks, I was so homesick I thought I couldn't bear it," she said.

Such was Cherry's first meeting with Meg. Father and daughter finally took notice of Cherry, who had been too startled to move. Sir Ian introduced the two: "The grandest nurse and the grandest daughter a man ever had."

Cherry and Meg regarded each other for a long moment. Each girl liked what she saw. And Sir Ian lay there and admired the pair: Meg with wavy brown hair; violet eyes, honest and sparkling with humor; fine regular features, friendly mouth, and as slim as a young willow. Cherry with glossy dark curls; dark, expressive eyes; red cheeks, and slender figure. What a beautiful picture they made! Renoir would have loved to paint them.

The two girls broke into smiles and shook hands warmly.

It was the beginning of a friendship which Cherry and Meg were to treasure. And it was the day which drew Cherry into the web of mystery of Balfour Island. For Meg had come determined to take her father home as soon as possible.

"He'll never get well," Meg told Dr. Joe and Cherry. "I know Da. He will worry a little more today, a little less tomorrow perhaps, but he'll never be at ease until he returns to the island. Something is wrong, though he won't tell me what it is. And he must see to it."

Because of Sir Ian's pattern of brief improvement, followed by a setback, Dr. Joe was inclined to agree. But he had to be sure Sir Ian had consistent and proper nursing care. Dr. Mackenzie had told him there were two registered nurses on the island, neither of whom could be spared from the island's hospital.

Both Sir Ian and Meg pleaded every day with Cherry to return with them. Sir Ian became stubborn and insisted he would not tolerate another nurse.

It was a big decision for Cherry to make.

"You'd not do wrong in going," Dr. Joe said, and

her family agreed. "I think," Dr. Joe had added, "it will be an interesting experience for you in many ways. I've made inquiries about young Dr. Douglas Mackenzie and all the reports are good. His reputation as a physician is excellent."

The moment Cherry said "Yes," Meg got on the long-distance telephone and began making arrangements with the servants at Barclay House for getting everything in order. Dr. Joe helped make arrangements with Hilton Hospital for Cherry's leave of absence. Cherry herself hurried around when off duty, buying all the things she "absolutely needed," and doing all the other things that had to be done when anyone plans to be away for several months.

"I surely hope all of this is not premature," her mother said to Cherry. "Dr. Joe hasn't said Sir Ian is well enough to travel."

"Oh, but Sir Ian has been improving steadily since Meg declared she was going to take him home and there's no hitch any longer about nursing care," Cherry told her. "Do you know, Sir Ian never even batted an eyelash when Meg told him Lloyd had already gone to the island? She was worried about breaking the news to him, as Lloyd had asked her to do. But she need not have worried at all. Sir Ian even told Meg to wire him to meet us as soon as we know when we will arrive."

"Well, as Dr. Joe told us the other evening when he came over," Mrs. Ames said, "he's known of patients who got over their ulcers on the first day of vacation. Sir Ian probably feels the same sort of relief."

CHAPTER VI

Balfour Island

IT WAS A RATHER COMPLICATED JOURNEY TO BAL-
four Island. From Hilton, Cherry, Sir Ian, and Meg
went by train to Chicago, and from there by plane to
St. John's, Newfoundland, in Canada. From there,
they took the ferryboat *Sandy Fergus* that ran between St. John's and the island.

The journey was further complicated, because Sir
Ian was a sick man and special arrangements had to
be made to ensure his comfort and to avoid fatigue.
Modern conveniences of travel made this a relatively
easy matter.

But Sir Ian's eagerness to get home made him
impatient and cross with those very precautions which
were taken for his health and comfort. During the
journey, it was all Cherry could do (aided by Meg)
to keep him reasonably calm and see that he followed
Dr. Joe's orders as cheerfully as possible.

The girls succeeded better perhaps than they re-

alized, for when the plane landed at St. John's, Newfoundland, just ahead of a fog, Sir Ian was actually
complacent about taking the slower, ancient ferryboat instead of the much faster helicopter to the island.

"The helicopter will never make it," Meg had said
at first signs of the fog.

"Ay," Sir Ian had agreed. "But you can depend
on John Rab getting us there, which is more than I
can say for the fal-de-lal whirlybirds."

John Rab was the captain and owner of the *Sandy
Fergus* ferryboat, and, as Cherry was to discover, let
neither fog, rain, wind, snowstorm, nor ice in Balmaghie Bay keep him from his two daily trips between
St. John's and Balfour.

The helicopter which carried mail and passengers
once a day, or on special flights, was faster. But it was
far less reliable. It supplied service only during fair
weather. Wind and fog made it impossible to land on
the island. Since fogs often hung over Balfour and
came at unexpected times, the Balfourians referred
to the helicopter as the "May Bee," which some wit
had named it, explaining, "Maybe you go and maybe
you don't. It all depends on the weather."

When Cherry, Sir Ian, and Meg got off the plane
at St. John's the fog was rolling in, dimming the
morning sun. The air was chilly. Cherry was glad she
had on her warm coat and had brought along woolen
sweaters, cardigans, and other warm clothing which
Meg had advised packing.

Sir Ian was bundled up. Cherry had insisted upon

it in spite of his protests. But she could see that both he and Meg were much happier with the colder climate. They had begun to find the spring weather in Hilton warm enough for their taste.

"The summer would be much too hot for us Newfoundlanders," Meg had told Cherry. "We'd melt."

Lloyd Barclay was waiting for them at the St. John's airport.

"Hello, everybody!" he greeted them. He shook hands with Cherry and gave Meg a cousinly peck on the cheek. "It's good to see you, sir," he said to his uncle, as they shook hands. "I have a taxi waiting to take us to the wharf. We'll have to ride the ferry. I came over in the May Bee, but the pilot didn't want to try to make it back."

Lloyd managed the meeting with such ease that one would have thought he was simply greeting them upon their return from a pleasant week end. All three of the Barclays behaved as though nothing unusual had happened during the past weeks. As for Cherry, she was consumed with curiosity about what Lloyd had found out upon his return to Balfour.

After luggage had been checked through customs and they were settled in the taxi, a converted limousine, Cherry thought surely Sir Ian or Lloyd, or Meg, at least, would ask Lloyd what had happened on the island. But Cherry was disappointed. They chatted casually of the trip and the weather.

Upon arrival at the wharf, Sir Ian permitted Lloyd to help him out of the car, then brushed away his nephew's helping hand, and started toward the boat.

He walked beside Lloyd with slow, deliberate steps, his shoulders back, his head high.

Cherry and Meg followed and, behind them, trailed the porters with bags and luggage.

"The king returns," ran through Cherry's mind. Sir Ian might be sick, but "his people" were not to see him leaning upon anyone's arm. That he had a nurse with him was of no importance. Sir Ian Barclay was able to have a dozen nurses if it so pleased him.

They made quite a swath down the middle of the wharf, through the crowd of people, past boxes and crates, for the wharf was busy. All along the way, their appearance was greeted with nods and "Good morning to you" from various people. Cherry, in her distinguishing nurse's attire, drew considerable attention, too. Undoubtedly people were curious about her being with the Barclays.

The *Sandy Fergus* was tied up at some distance down the wharf. They passed small vessels moored alongside and could see through the mist the shapes of tankers, fishing boats, and ships anchored in the harbor.

At last they reached the ferryboat and were met, as they stepped aboard, by the captain, John Rab, a grizzled-headed old sea dog with a pipe in his mouth.

"I've been expecting ye," he said, gripping Sir Ian's hand in his big paw. "Told Lloyd I'd hold the boat if need be. Welcome home, Ian."

This was the first time Cherry had heard the mine owner called anything but *Sir* Ian.

The captain was obviously delighted to see Sir Ian and Meg, and they to see him. When Cherry was introduced, he gave her a sharp look from under shaggy eyebrows.

"A fine lass of a nurse, eh?" he said in a deep, singing Scottish voice. "I'm glad ye've come." He jerked his head toward Sir Ian. "This old chap here can do with a bit of looking after. Ulcers are pawky things."

"The captain means they're stubborn," Sir Ian growled amiably. "He still talks the way he did when we were in school together in Scotland."

While they were talking to the captain, the boat had been gradually taking on passengers. There were forty or so men, women, and children scattered about the deck and leaning against the rail of the old fishing vessel. That is what the *Sandy Fergus* had been originally. And, indeed, Captain Rab still used it for occasional fishing, as was quite evident from the odor.

A deck hand came to report to Captain Rab that a place in the cabin had been arranged where Sir Ian and his party would be comfortable.

As they moved toward the cabin, Cherry felt herself jostled. Turning her head, she saw a man hurrying past in a group of latecomers, for it was within a few minutes of departure time. The man stopped suddenly a little ahead of them. He was a short, powerful little man, with a dark hat pulled down at an angle. He was dressed in a gray suit, a bit too obviously expensive to be in the best of taste.

He saw Cherry glance at him through the cabin window as she sat down inside, and moved quickly out of sight.

Sir Ian, settled comfortably on the window seat, was immediately surrounded by well-wishers who had been on business, shopping trips, or visits to relatives on the mainland.

Cherry would have retired to the background, but Sir Ian kept bringing her forward to introduce her to one more of the returning islanders.

Far from being annoyed by the fuss made over him, Sir Ian was enjoying himself hugely. He was rather like a king holding court. And he was genuinely interested in what everyone had to say. He knew all about their families and plied them with questions.

Hearing them talk, Cherry felt that she had been dropped into a corner of Scotland. In fact, as Lloyd had once said to her, "Balfour and its people are a bit of Scotland, only separated, of course, by the Atlantic Ocean."

It was all very warm and friendly between Sir Ian and his visitors. But Cherry observed that things were not the same between him and a little, wiry, white-haired lady, accompanied by a skinny, tow-headed boy about ten or eleven years old.

When Cherry had entered the cabin, she had heard the boy ask, "Grandma, aren't we going in to see Sir Ian and Miss Meg?"

"Oh, dear, no! We'll not be troubling them," the elderly woman had answered, and hustled the boy away.

Now and then, Cherry caught sight of the two walking up and down the deck or leaning against the rail outside.

During a period when Sir Ian and Meg were in lively conversation with their visitors, Lloyd suggested to Cherry that she might like to take a turn around the deck.

"I'd love to," she told him.

"Meg will look after Uncle Ian," he said. "Besides, nobody will miss us when they have their lord and lady of the manor."

"Why, Lloyd, you sound bitter," Cherry said, as he guided her outside.

"Not really," he replied. "It's just that I've been away so long, at school and working in the States, that people here treat me rather like a stranger."

They walked to the bow of the boat and stood gazing at the rough water. Waves rolled in white plumes off the sides and cast salt spray in their faces. The mist, like tattered veils, trailed over the boat and the water. It was rather as though they were floating in space.

"I think I love the sea," Cherry said musingly.

"You'll make a good Balfourian," Lloyd complimented her, "if you can enjoy the sea and the fog. That's the first test. But wait until we have a clear, sunny day. You'll really love it then. This narrow passage between Balmaghie Bay on the west and the Atlantic Ocean on the east—we're crossing it now— is always rough. Never much quieter than this. And in bad weather, of course, the water rushes through like a torrent. In fine weather, though, Balmaghie Bay is calm and blue and the Atlantic grows quieter. The island lies between the bay and the sea, rising out of the waters like a jewel." Lloyd broke off suddenly. "Sorry, Cherry," he apologized. "I get carried away. I didn't mean to give you a lecture on natural history."

Lloyd watched the water alongside the boat a bit, then said abruptly, "Cherry, remember the story in the newspaper?"

"Oh, my!" she exclaimed, laughing. "I wondered when you were going to say something about that. How could I forget it? I've practically bitten my tongue off to keep from asking questions. The story of the explosion brought you flying back here."

"You are right," Lloyd said. He grinned ruefully at her and went on, "Well, it was a tempest in a tea-pot. The explosion, that is. For some reason, probably someone's carelessness, there was a small, delayed blast in Number 2 mine just after the miners had knocked off work. It did some damage in one of the tunnels."

"But it might have injured some of the men," said Cherry.

"It might," agreed Lloyd. "Though there are safety measures which probably would have prevented it. I've been investigating our safety methods. Some of the miners aren't nearly as careful as they should be."

"Isn't it strange that all the trouble has been in Number 2 mine?" asked Cherry. "What does Mr. Cameron say?"

"Well, Jock can't explain it," replied Lloyd. "In fact, he was quite evasive about the whole thing. I couldn't seem to get a direct answer out of him. I don't know what in the world has happened to him. He actually avoids me. And every day he has off he goes fishing. That may not sound unusual to you because you expect people on an island to go fishing. But not Old Jock. He used to sail his boat on Sundays in summer in Balmaghie Bay. When I was a boy, he would take me and some of the other boys sailing. But he never cared much about fishing. Now, every chance he gets, out in that rowboat he goes. And he doesn't go in the bay; he goes out in the ocean, deep-sea fishing not far from our big sea cave we call Rogues' Cave. As they say in Scotland, I don't know what's come over the man."

"What about McGuire?" asked Cherry. "I thought you rushed up here to give McGuire a piece of your mind."

"That was the idea," Lloyd admitted. "But that young fellow appears to know his business. He's from the new iron mines in northern Quebec and he brought a good crew with him. Broderick recommended him, incidentally. I did start to tear into him about giving out the statement to the press on the explosion and telling Uncle Ian about the weakened walls in the tunnel of Number 2 mine. Then he explained that Mr. Cameron was off on those days and he was technically in charge. And, of course, the man was right. I respect McGuire's skill as a miner and his ability to handle a mining crew, but I can't say I like him particularly," Lloyd confessed. "He's too aggressive and extremely ambitious."

"Perhaps that's why Mr. Cameron is behaving so strangely," suggested Cherry. "Wouldn't you be angry and terribly hurt if you were in his place? A younger man is brought in, an ambitious fellow, and

Mr. Cameron feels he is being pushed out of his job."

"Oh, Old Jock—everyone calls him that—knows that Uncle Ian would never let that happen," declared Lloyd. "But Old Jock's nose undoubtedly is out of joint over McGuire and he's being stubborn and uncooperative—that's about what it amounts to and I'll have to bear with him for the time being."

"Well, please don't tell your uncle about all this just now," Cherry cautioned. "He's in no condition to be excited or worried about anything."

Lloyd patted her hand and smiled engagingly at her. "There now, I'll always be as soft as a kitten with the old tyrant. So don't get the wind up, nurse lass. Haven't I behaved well so far?" He tweaked one of her curls.

"No complaints so far," she said, grinning. Just then, she saw the little old lady and the boy and plucked Lloyd's sleeve. "Who are they?" she asked quickly.

"Who? Where?" Lloyd swiveled his head about.

"Oh, dear! You can't see them now. They're behind all those other people," Cherry told him. "It's an old lady and a boy. The boy wanted to see your uncle, but his grandmother wouldn't let him. She doesn't seem to like him much."

"Maybe she *doesn't* like Uncle Ian," said Lloyd, laughing. "Some people have been known not to like him, you know. He can be a grizzly bear at times. Scares people, makes them mad."

"Well, I'm sure he doesn't go around frightening old ladies and little boys," scoffed Cherry. "I think I'd better go back. It's my responsibility to see that your uncle doesn't tire himself out. And just let him try being a grizzly bear to scare me," she boasted with mock severity, "and I'll clobber him."

"That's the way to talk," said Lloyd. "Well, where you go, I go, pretty maid." He took her arm with a gallant air and escorted her back to the cabin.

It was not long before they reached Balfour. The distance from St. John's was about four miles or so, but the time varied with the state of the weather. The *Sandy Fergus* on good days in fair seas could cross in under an hour. On bad days it was hard to tell how long the crossing would take. Today, the boat had made good time. Captain Rab considered the fog too slight to be worthy of the name.

Standing on deck, Cherry saw Balfour Island when it was at neither its best nor its worst. The noonday sun, shining through the mist, gave a milky sort of light. The breeze off the island smelled of balsam and pine. There was a view of the sandy beach of the harbor, the wharves, boats, and little frame houses. Back of them were trees and the network of conveyors and bridges and power lines of the mines. They formed a lacy pattern on ridges and hills and above the little valleys.

"There!" Meg was saying and prodding Cherry. "Up there on the cliffs to the right is Barclay House. That's where we're going. It faces the ocean on one side and Balmaghie Bay on the other."

Cherry looked up to the gray walls of the big house, with its square tower, balconies, and tall chimneys, like a castle, atop the cliff.

"How beautiful!" Cherry exclaimed. "Makes me think of gallant knights and fair ladies."

The *Sandy Fergus* drew alongside the wharf. In a moment, then, they were going ashore—Lloyd close to his uncle and Cherry and Meg behind. There was

"Up there on the cliffs is Barclay House!"

a little crowd of men, women, and children on the wharf.

There were cheers for Sir Ian. Some called out greetings to Meg and Lloyd. Youngsters waved. Everyone stared at Cherry attentively, interested as people in a small community always are in a stranger.

Two men detached themselves from the crowd—a lanky, sandy-haired young man with a pleasantly ugly face; and a big, jovial, red-faced, red-haired man with prominent blue eyes. They shook hands with the Barclays, then Meg introduced them to Cherry. Dr. Douglas Mackenzie was the lanky one and Michael McGuire the big fellow, who, judging from his build, had probably played end on a college football team.

Cherry's impression on seeing Dr. Mackenzie was one of surprise. From hearing Sir Ian and Dr. Joe talk about him (Dr. Joe had got his impression from the man's voice over the phone), Cherry had imagined the doctor as a very young, very studious and earnest type of fellow with horn-rimmed glasses. Then, too, she had expected him to be quite reserved and formal.

But he was not in the least what she had imagined. He was not very young. She thought he was between thirty and thirty-five. His manner was easy and informal; his bony face was wonderfully kind; he wore no glasses and his large brown eyes were keenly observant.

"I like him," Cherry thought. "I think we'll get on together."

Because he was Sir Ian's physician, she would have to work under Dr. Mackenzie's direction. If the doctor were a difficult person, her nursing job could be made quite trying. Cherry worked well with most people, even temperamental ones. But it was always easier to work with those who had agreeable personalities. She liked Dr. Mackenzie very much indeed on sight. And it was plain to be seen that he and Meg were very much in love. They could scarcely take their eyes off each other.

"Where's Jock Cameron?" Sir Ian demanded all of a sudden.

"I saw him take his boat out early this morning," piped up a man in the crowd. "He's probably gone fishing."

"Gone fishing?" Sir Ian cried in amazement. Turning to McGuire, he asked, "Wasn't he in the office this morning?"

"Oh, well, it's Old Jock's day off and he's gone fishing," McGuire answered.

"You're a fine one to be asking for Jock Cameron, Sir Ian," cried a thin, quavery voice, and a wisp of a man advanced slowly toward the mine owner. "Ye think a man's got no pride? He dinna take it kindly that ye've seen fit to make certain changes in operating the mines. Bringing in a young sprout from Quebec to lord it over him." The man glanced at McGuire with dislike.

Sir Ian glared down at the little old man. "Just what do you mean talking such stuff and nonsense, Tim Morgan?" he demanded angrily.

Dr. Mackenzie moved quickly and laid a gentle hand on Tim Morgan's shoulder. "You must excuse Sir Ian now, Mr. Morgan," the doctor said. "After he's rested, I'm sure he'll be glad to see you."

Cherry stepped to Sir Ian's side, and putting her hand on his elbow, propelled him firmly but gently toward the foot of the wharf where the chauffeur stood beside the open door of the Barclays' not-very-new Rolls-Royce.

"Sir Ian has had an exhausting trip," she said crisply to McGuire and those gathered around. "He must go home and get some rest at once."

Dr. Mackenzie, Sir Ian, Cherry, Lloyd, and Meg walked to the car. The chauffeur started the motor. They drove off up High Street that led from the waterfront, through the village, climbing up and up to Barclay House on the cliffs.

~~~~~~

CHAPTER VII

Island Nurse

IT WAS THE MIDDLE OF THE AFTERNOON WHEN
Cherry finally went downstairs to lunch. Sir Ian was
in an agitated state and refused point-blank to go to
bed and rest. Dr. Mackenzie, or Dr. Mac as everyone
called him on Balfour, was friendly but firm, shooed
everyone away but Cherry, and got Sir Ian into bed.
By that time Sir Ian was glad to go, for he had too
much pain to stir about.

Dr. Mac gave him medication to relieve any acid
condition in his stomach. Cherry gave him a feeding
of milk and cream to which he reacted well.

Between little twitches of pain, Sir Ian complained
and grumbled. He had come back, he said, to look
after his mines and how was he going to do it if some
young whippersnapper of a doctor and a mere lass of
a nurse kept him in bed? Couldn't they see that everything was at sixes and sevens on the island?

Dr. Mac listened gravely, nodding in agreement to
everything the mine owner said.

"Weel, why don't you say something, Mackenzie?" Sir Ian burst out at last in exasperation.

The doctor grinned, his face wrinkling in amusement. "Why, sir, you didn't give me a chance," he replied.

"Weel, then, why didn't you stop me?" demanded the other irascibly. "No, you sat bobbing your head like a silly nuthatch pecking open a nut. And you, Cherry, what was the matter with you?"

"I agreed with Dr. Mac's unvoiced opinion," Cherry said primly. "It was better to let you get it off your chest. Perhaps now you'll settle down and get some rest."

"Ye are a red-cheeked tyrant," Sir Ian accused her. "Ye wait. When I get well, I'll show ye who's boss."

"Unless you quit upsetting yourself over things you can do nothing about," said Dr. Mac, "you are going to lie there and be a milksop. Isn't that correct, Miss Ames?"

"Absolutely, Doctor," Cherry agreed with vigor.

"Ought never to get sick," grumbled Sir Ian, turning his head aside and closing his eyes. "Lose your independence. Have to do as you're bid."

Sir Ian pretended to sleep for a while. When the pain left, he began to doze. The trip had tired him.

"Call me at the hospital," Dr. Mac told Cherry on leaving, "if you need me for anything. But I'll be back later, anyway, to see how he is."

Cherry sat alone with Sir Ian for a while longer, then Meg peeked in to say that she would relieve her.

"You must have lunch, Cherry," Meg told her. "Lloyd and I had ours ages ago, then he went down to the mines. I'll stay with father. I had Higgins lay a place in the dining room and keep the chops warm. If you don't like lamb chops, just tell Higgins and he'll have Tess—that's the cook—fix you something you do like."

Robert Higgins was the family's butler.

"Thank you, Meg. A lamb chop will do nicely," Cherry assured her. "I'll not take long."

Cherry left, going into her own room across the hall for a moment to freshen up. The family's bedrooms and the guest rooms were all on the second floor. Cherry's room was on the northeast corner of the house, overlooking the cliffs above a great cave, called Rogues' Cave, in the cliffside.

From the east windows, Cherry had a magnificent view of the cliffs and the sea. On the north, the windows looked out over the island and onto the big hill where iron ore had first been discovered on the island and the first mine located well over a hundred years before. That mine had been worked out and abandoned long ago. The top of the hill where the entrance to the mine shaft had once been was grown over now with bushes and vines.

Cherry stood for a minute gazing at the scene, then walked down the long hall, down the curving staircase, to the center hall below, where portraits of generations of Barclays looked down upon her. Some were grim and stern, others smiled aloofly. Meg resembled one of the ladies very much. The difference was in the dress which told Cherry that Meg would have had to be a hundred and fifty years old to have posed for the artist.

"This way, Miss Ames," Higgins said, suddenly appearing in front of her. The butler was old-fashioned and formal without being stiff. He had served the Barclays since Meg's father was a young man. And his father and his grandfather before him had been butlers to the Barclays. Higgins led Cherry across the hall, past the west drawing room and into the dining room, filled with heavy mahogany and teak furniture.

As he was serving her lunch, she asked, "Higgins, why is the cave in the cliff below my windows called Rogues' Cave?"

"I heard from my grandda that it was once a hide-out for smugglers, Miss Ames," he answered.

"Oh! What did they smuggle?"

"Brandy and whisky for traders who exchanged them with the Indians for furs," Higgins said, shaking his head in disapproval.

"Does anyone ever go spelunking? I mean, does anybody go exploring the cave?" asked Cherry, helping herself to more of the chutney for the lamb.

"Not that I know of, Miss Ames," he replied. "Not far inside anyway since Sir Ian, that is, the old Sir Ian—the present Sir Ian's father and Miss Meg's grandfather—was a boy. My da said that the boy was lost for three days in Rogues' Cave. Delirious when they found him on the beach, raving of gold and silver and crying 'Open sesame!' Of course, the boy's head was filled with tales of adventure, for all he was a little scientist."

"A scientist?" Cherry asked.

"Ay. My da was fond of telling me how little Sir

Ian used the room at the top of the tower for his experiments," Higgins told her. "He was always crushing stones and melting things down in his little furnace. At the same time, he liked to imagine himself a Barbary pirate, a prince of Araby, an Indian chief, or whatever struck his fancy when he wasn't mixing and boiling and cooking his chemical formulas."

"He must have been a very unusual and imaginative boy," Cherry commented.

"He was that, Miss Ames," Higgins agreed. "Then he would sit up there in the tower"—he motioned in the general direction of the square, stone tower at the end of the house—"writing in what he called his 'Secret Journal' by candlelight at night."

"It would be fascinating to see what he wrote," Cherry said. "Perhaps Sir Ian might let me look at the journal."

"No one but the boy ever laid eyes on it to anyone's knowledge," replied Higgins. "He kept it hidden away. Then I dare say by the time he returned from schooling in Scotland he had forgot all about it, for my da told me that the master of Barclay House never spoke of it more, once he took up the management of the mines."

"So no one ever saw it," said Cherry. "That's too bad."

"Ay. But the tower room is almost the same now as when the old Sir Ian was a boy," the butler told her. "The present Sir Ian never disturbed anything, for he was not interested in experiments. He was concerned only about operating the mines."

Having finished her lunch, Cherry thanked Higgins for his interesting conversation and went upstairs. Through the open door of Sir Ian's room, Meg's and her father's voices floated down the hall. The acoustics were such that the hallway acted as an amplifier and Cherry could hear more distinctly than if she were in the room with them.

"Da, dear, you mustn't be cross with Aunt Phyllis," Meg was saying. "I had the money, so I offered it to her. She's terribly broke and in debt. It's so frightfully expensive living in London and having the two boys off in school. She has a dreadful time; she just can't make ends meet."

"Never could. A sieve as far as money is concerned," observed Sir Ian. "My sister Phyllis is the spoiled baby of the family. She's been a widow long enough. Ought to get married again. Solve all her problems."

Meg laughed. "Suppose she picked a poor man, then you would be in the soup, wouldn't you? You'd have to support her husband, too."

Sir Ian grunted. "And that younger brother of mine, your uncle George. You saw him in London. He wanted me to give him another advance on his income, no doubt," he said.

"Well, Da, the mines haven't been paying a great deal for several years," Meg pointed out. "Uncle George has always been used to living like a gentleman of wealth and now he hasn't enough income to cover his expenses. He keeps falling behind a little more each year, just like Aunt Phyllis."

Sir Ian grunted again. "Your uncle George might quit living like a gentleman of wealth—a playboy to put it more accurately—and go to work," he remarked dryly.

"I don't suppose you could let Aunt Phyllis and Uncle George have some money to tide them over, could you, Da?" Meg pleaded.

"Not a penny," her father said with finality. "Haven't got it to give. They'll have to whistle for it somewhere else this time."

Although Cherry could not help overhearing their conversation, she did not like to be eavesdropping on the Barclays' family affairs. Money problems were always embarrassing to people. Sir Ian's younger brother and sister, she gathered, expected to live in luxury in England on income from their shares in the Balfour Mines.

Apparently out of the present Barclay family, the only one who was really interested in the mines was Lloyd. Meg had told her that Lloyd's father and mother had lived at Barclay House until their death in an earthquake when they were on a trip to the Pacific islands six years before. Lloyd's father was next in age to Sir Ian, who was the eldest in the family. The two brothers had divided the operation of the mines between them. They had made a wonderful team, and his brother's death had been a terrible blow to Sir Ian.

"I admire his courage, trying to carry on alone," Cherry thought. "Sir Ian's brother and sister are actually dependent on his operating the mines, and they're always wanting money. Goodness knows how many other difficulties the poor man has. I don't wonder he has ulcers. Maybe Lloyd will be of help to him. If Sir Ian will let him—that's the thing."

Cherry entered her own room, and going into the bathroom, washed her hands, making a great splash of water so they would know that she had come upstairs. When she came out, Meg was just getting up from her chair in Sir Ian's bedroom. "Here's Cherry," Meg said. "So I'll run along to the library, Da. I promised to take over the story hour every afternoon. Is there anything you want me to bring you from the village?"

"Can't think of anything," replied her father. "Suppose you're going to stop by the hospital, too."

"Trying to make me blush, you old fraud," cried Meg, making a face at him. "You know perfectly well Douglas Mackenzie, M.D., is coming here later and he's staying on for dinner." She blew a kiss to her father from the doorway and was gone.

The rest of the afternoon was quiet. Higgins brought Cherry tea about six o'clock. She had had lunch too late to eat anything, although the little cakes and sandwiches looked very tempting.

At six thirty Lloyd came upstairs to look in on his uncle. "How's the old boy doing?" he whispered to Cherry.

"All right," she whispered back. "He hasn't complained of pain for some time."

Lloyd regarded Cherry concernedly. "You must be worn out," he observed. "You've lost all that lovely red in your cheeks. Don't you want to lie down and get some rest before dinner? Because you're going to have dinner with us downstairs. I've already asked Norah—she's the housemaid—to look in on Uncle once in a while."

"Bossy type, aren't you, Lloyd Barclay?" Cherry teased him. "I'm perfectly fine, but I think I could do with some air. After I've seen the doctor, I will take a walk outside, if I'm not needed."

"Doc's on his way up now," Lloyd said.

A few minutes later Cherry had put on her brown suede jacket and gone outdoors, for Dr. Mackenzie had not kept her.

She had a chance to examine the big house. It sat near the edge of the cliffs on the east, but there were gardens at the back and a greenhouse. On the west side, there was a garage and more gardens. In front were lawns and shrubbery. Two gateposts, although there was neither gate nor fence, marked the entrance to the broad drive that curved before the front door. The house was three stories high. The tower was five stories. Meg had told her that the servants' quarters were on the third floor toward the rear. The tower interested Cherry and she noticed that it could be entered from the outside. There was a tiny door, almost hidden by the masonry, in the north wall. On impulse, Cherry tried the door, but it was locked.

She walked idly up the hill toward the abandoned mine. Beyond was a little patch of balsam fir, but upon the rounded hill nothing grew but stiff grass, vines, and bushes among outcroppings of rock.

Cherry was halfway up the hill when, to her great surprise, a man rose from one of the outcroppings and confronted her.

"Who are you?" the man demanded

"What are you doing here?" he demanded. "Who are you?"

"My name is Cherry Ames. I'm Sir Ian Barclay's nurse," she answered. "I'm out for a walk, that's all."

He apologized gruffly. "I'm Jock Cameron," he told her. "That name mean anything to you?"

"It certainly does," Cherry assured him. "You're the superintendent of the Balfour Mines and an old friend of Sir Ian. In fact, you and he grew up on Balfour." She paused. "Now . . . let's . . . see. Oh, yes! The Barclays and the Camerons came over with forty families to settle Balfour Island in 1750. The Camerons had been the trusted stewards of the Barclay lands for generations in Scotland. At first, Balfour Island was a fishing colony, then when iron was discovered in eighteen hundred and . . ."

"Stop, before the breath of ye goes out," interrupted Jock Cameron, his manner becoming cordial. "Ye have heard of me, I see that weel."

Jock Cameron was a short, stocky man, dressed in fisherman's rough clothes. A canvas tote bag, which served as his creel, hung over his shoulder, although he had no other fishing gear with him. He regarded Cherry steadily for a bit. Then, with a quick gesture, he pushed his hat to the back of his head, revealing bushy, ginger hair.

"Tell me, nurse lass, how sick is he?" he asked suddenly.

"Sir Ian was desperately sick when they brought him into the hospital at Hilton," Cherry said.

"He dinna tell me that in his letter," Mr. Cameron said.

"I know he didn't," Cherry said. "I wrote that letter for him and mailed it."

"He's better now?" he asked.

Cherry nodded. "Yes, quite a bit better."

"Good," Jock Cameron said, nodding with satisfaction.

With that, he turned quickly and started away. Then, stopping and wheeling around, he came back. "Do not say to anyone—anyone at all—ye saw Old Jock Cameron on the hill this night," he said softly. "Promise ye'll not tell."

His eyes searched her face, waiting for her answer. What there was about the man that made her trust him suddenly, Cherry did not know. But she heard herself saying, "I won't tell."

He seemed satisfied, and, turning once more, walked away out of sight over the crest of the hill.

Late that night Cherry was to wonder if she had not been too hasty.

Sir Ian was asleep. She had gone into her own room for a while.

She stood at the window, thinking how lovely it was outside. The fog had lifted. The sky was clear and the stars were out. A movement on the front lawn caught her eye.

At first she thought it was a large dog crossing the lawn close to the shrubbery. Upon reaching the wall near the corner of the house, the figure raised up and she realized it was a man who had been running crouched over. Now he ran along, hugging the wall, and was soon out of her range of vision. She had the impression, though, that the man was Jock Cameron.

CHAPTER VIII

The Sea Cave

NEXT MORNING, MEG LEFT FOR ST. JOHN'S TO DO some extensive marketing and shopping for the house. She expected to be gone a couple of days or so.

It took good management to keep a household the size of the Barclays' running efficiently. Meg managed it so effortlessly that no one was aware of how much time and thought she spent in making everything operate smoothly. She had even taken on an extra maid—an older woman with some experience in practical nursing—for the few days she would be away, so that Cherry would have proper relief from duty.

Lloyd left early in the morning for the mines and did not return all day. It was late in the evening before he came in, tired, to go immediately to his room. Either in the morning or the evening, or both, he would peek in on his uncle to see how he was.

Cherry, who could not get the mysterious figure on the lawn out of her mind, would have asked Lloyd about it, but he was so absorbed in his work and always in such a hurry that she did not like to bother him.

Thus it was not until several days had passed that she had a chance to tell Meg about seeing the man in the moonlight.

Meg laughed. "You probably caught one of the fishermen going down to our private beach," she told Cherry. "They aren't supposed to use it. There are any number of other beaches, but once in a while one sneaks down."

That explained someone crossing the lawn that night. Cherry's impression that the man was Jock Cameron was, after all, she realized, only an impression.

The day after Meg got back from St. John's, Sir Ian had a good morning. Lloyd came to the house for lunch instead of having it at the staff dining room at the Mine Office. He reported to his uncle that he expected No. 2 mine to go into operation soon. No. 2 was nearest the abandoned No. 1 Mine. McGuire agreed with Lloyd that No. 2, although well worked, could be profitably operated by modern methods.

Lloyd had really taken hold of his job as mining engineer. While his uncle had still been in Hilton Hospital, he had got under way a survey of the mines, the equipment, and facilities; studied the production and other reports; had assays made of ore from the different mines so that he would have a definite idea of the value. Now this news about No. 2 was unusually good.

Sir Ian was as pleased as Punch. It did him a world of good. He would not let on how happy it made him. He simply grunted and remarked to Cherry, "Young fellow's full of beans today, isn't he?"

Lloyd and Cherry grinned at each other.

"Yes, *sir*," agreed Cherry emphatically. "And what's more, I think Lloyd Barclay is having himself a whale of a good time."

When Norah, the maid, came to stay with Sir Ian that afternoon, Meg came to ask Cherry if she could show her the beach and the sea cave. "The cave's really quite fun," Meg said.

Cherry replied that, of course, she would be delighted.

They put on warm jackets because Meg said it would be chilly and damp down there. The two girls went out the front of the house, followed the narrow gravel path that led to the tower, and continued along the edge of the cliffs to stone steps cut in the rock. The steps started from the brow of the cliff and descended by turns and inclines to the foot, a hundred feet below.

Cherry looked down over the edge to the sea and to where the waves were frothing about some black rocks a little distance from shore. The rocks formed a natural breakwater and, inside, the sea at low tide as it was then, was as still as a lagoon. She could see a patch of white where the cliff curved inward, forming a little bay with a stretch of sandy beach.

"It's beautiful!" Cherry exclaimed.

"I think so," said Meg. "On the other side of the

rocks, the sea is very deep and there is good fishing. Shall we go on down?"

Cherry said she was ready. With Meg ahead, they started along the zigzag course that the steps made in the face of the cliff. Cherry felt almost as though she were a fly walking on a wall, for the rocky crag rose almost straight upward from the sea floor. It was windy on the cliffs. Their hair was whipped about and they could feel the tingle of damp salt air on their faces.

Although Meg tripped gaily in front of her with the ease of long familiarity, Cherry was glad to have the guard chain to hold on to. It ran through stout iron balusters embedded in the rock.

As they went down, they disturbed the gulls which took off with much screaming and a thunderous flapping of wings.

When they reached the bottom, they stepped directly upon the white sand of the beach. At each end of the beach, a jumble of rocks extended like arms into the sea.

At the north end there was a considerable distance between the breakwater and the arm of rocks.

"Room enough for a good-sized boat to get through there," Meg said, "when the tide is coming in. At the south end, the rocks jut far out into the sea and it's too dangerous to try to get into the little bay. Lloyd and I used to wait for the tide and maneuver our ketch in and out through the north passage when we were kids."

She started to walk up the beach. "Come along," she said to Cherry. "I'll show you the cave."

A few yards away was Rogues' Cave. Cherry and Meg looked up at the entrance which had been dug out by the action of the sea, and opened into the cavern. The archway was very high and wide.

"When the tide is in," Meg was saying as they entered the dim interior, "you can bring a motor launch in here. Look!" she cried. "Someone has left a rowboat moored inside. Probably belongs to that mysterious character you saw the other night." She laughed lightheartedly. "I've never known any of the fishermen to leave their boats before."

The floor of the cave was on the same level as the beach. On one side, up about ten or eleven feet, was a broad ledge with several iron ringbolts secured in the rock. To one of these, the rowboat was tied by a rope just long enough to permit the boat to rest on the cave floor. When the tide came in, of course, the boat floated to the height of the ledge. Cherry could see the marks left by the last high tide like a ring around the walls.

She was not too familiar with the handling of boats, but it struck her as odd to see the oarlocks wrapped with cloth.

Whoever had used the boat evidently had not wanted to make any noise, she concluded, so he had muffled the sound of the oars sliding in the locks.

"Hello, down there!" Cherry heard above her somewhere. Looking up to her left, she saw Meg poised like a pretty water sprite, on the rocky ledge. "Come on up," Meg invited. "Use the steps down there at the end."

Cherry found the steps, climbed up, and she and

Meg walked along the ledge toward the rear of the cavern where there was an opening in the rocks and more steps going up. These vanished in complete darkness.

"Now I'll show you my special treat, if you don't mind a little dirt," Meg said, beginning to mount the stairs.

"We'll have to turn into night owls to see anything, I should think," Cherry told her with a laugh. "It's pitch black up there."

"Meg of the Mounties is never unprepared," declared the other. "I have brought with me my faithful flashlight, as you Americans call it." She snapped it on.

"And what do you Canadians call it?" asked Cherry as she started to follow Meg and the yellow circle of light.

"Flashlight," replied Meg gaily. "Every time Aunt Phyllis used the English term torch for flashlight I had visions of a medieval character bearing aloft a burning torch."

The steps led up to a sort of tunnel or corridor, which they walked along for several yards.

Then Meg stopped. "Here we are," she said, stooping over to examine the rocks in the wall to her right. She played the light over the wall for a minute or so. "Now, where is the thing, anyway?" She felt along the wall with her hand. "Oh, I've got it! See, Cherry, it's this little flat knob of stone."

"I see it," Cherry told her.

"Now, watch," ordered Meg. She pulled on it and a thin slab of rock grated noisily and swung outward, revealing an opening large enough for a person to enter. Meg promptly bent over and went inside. Cherry followed.

They found themselves in a narrow niche about six feet long and high enough for a not-too-tall man to stand upright without bumping his head.

"It's the smugglers' old hidey-hole," explained Meg. "Isn't it wonderfully eerie? Lloyd and I discovered it one summer ever so long ago. We never told a soul. We kept it a deep, dark secret."

"My, it certainly is eerie," agreed Cherry, eying the ancient stones, gray and cold. She could easily picture a smuggler armed with pistols and cutlass hiding from his pursuers.

"Gives me the same delicious shivers that reading a ghost story does," she said.

"Doesn't it," said Meg. She paused, cocking her head. "Listen!" She put a restraining hand on Cherry's arm. "I thought I heard something."

They both listened. A harsh sound as though of something scraping over stone or sand came to them from close by. Cherry, who was standing near the wall, smelled an overpowering odor of fish. The sound seemed to come closer. It was just outside. Just then, to the girls' astonishment, they saw the slab door of the niche closing. For a moment, they stood stock-still, watching with horrified eyes, the door moving inch by inch.

Cherry was first to act. Pushing Meg aside, she gave the door a tremendous kick. It swung open with a sort of shrieking scrape across the stones.

Meg leaned against Cherry and laughed weakly.

"Aren't we silly?" she asked. "We almost frightened ourselves out of our wits. You see there's a vent hole up above somewhere. When the wind blows in a certain direction, there's a great rush of air along this tunnel. The wind has veered since we came in the cave and the draft pushed the door shut. You see, Cherry, it was only the wind!" she said, flinging out her arm dramatically.

Cherry let out her breath with a puff. "Whee! I thought we were about to be held captive by pirates or no telling what," she said.

"Well, I promised you a special treat and you can't say I didn't give you one," Meg pointed out.

"At least I'll be prepared the next time you use the phrase," observed Cherry ruefully. "Incidentally, I think I'd better be getting back."

"You're the doctor—I mean the nurse," Meg replied. "I'd better be getting back myself. It's probably almost time for my story hour at the library." She bent down. "I suppose I'd better lead the way," she said and went with stooped back out the door. "Oh, dear!" she cried at once. "I've lost an earring. Will you see if I dropped it in there?" She handed Cherry the flashlight.

As Cherry stood with her back against the wall, she got another strong whiff of fish. She sniffed. It was definitely coming from the wall behind her. Turning around, she saw some kind of cloth tucked in a crevice between the stones. A corner stuck out and, on impulse, she gave it a tug. It had been stuffed in loosely and it came out at her first tug. She held in her hand a tote bag of canvas—a creel by the smell of it. Stamped in black ink on one side were the initials J. C.

"Jock Cameron's creel," thought Cherry, suppressing a gasp. "The day I saw him on the hill, he had one just like this. That night I saw him on the lawn he must have been on his way here. Had he hidden here? Why?" With these questions buzzing in her head, Cherry had not heard Meg calling her. Now she heard Meg almost shouting her name.

"Can't you find the earring?" cried Meg.

Cherry thrust the tote bag under her arm.

"I'm hunting," she sang out to Meg, and played the flashlight into the corners of the hidey-hole. There was a glint and Cherry pounced. "Here it is!" she exclaimed. She crouched over and made her way through the door.

"Thank you, Cherry, I'm awfully glad you found it," Meg said when they were outside the hidey-hole. "I just couldn't bear losing another. I have more unmatched earrings than anyone I know."

She paused, sniffing, then exclaimed, "Goodness! Where is that strong fishy odor coming from?"

"From this," Cherry said, holding the tote bag up to the beam of the flashlight. "You see, I found something besides your earring in the hidey-hole."

Meg examined it, looking closely at the initials J. C. "Now, what do you suppose Old Jock Cameron was doing in that hidey-hole?" she said, puzzled.

"You recognize this tote bag?" Cherry cried.

Meg shook her head. "No, that was only a calculated guess," she admitted. "But that's the kind of a creel some fishermen use. And Lloyd was telling me about Old Jock going fishing on his days off. The tote bag has J. C. on it. Taken altogether, it seemed to add up to Jock Cameron." She sighed. "And I practically just got through telling you, Cherry, that Lloyd and I had kept the hidey-hole a deep, dark secret. But here's evidence that our cherished childhood secret has been discovered by someone. And that someone probably is Old Jock." Meg ended on a mock-tragic note, and sighed deeply.

"Why do you suppose he, if it were Mr. Cameron, left the creel in there?" asked Cherry.

"Oh, he leaves it here, so he'll have it when he goes fishing, I suppose," replied Meg.

"I suppose I'd better put it back where I found it, in any case," Cherry said.

Meg giggled and held her nose delicately. "Yes, put it back quickly."

Cherry ducked into the hidey-hole and stuffed the creel again into the crevice. Outside once more, with the door to the hidey-hole closed, Cherry said, "If that *was* Mr. Cameron's creel, do you suppose that is his boat we saw tied up when we came into the cave?"

"With muffled oarlocks?" said Meg, starting back toward the cave entrance, with Cherry following after her. "Oh, no, I don't think so, unless . . ."

Before she could finish, Cherry interrupted. "So you noticed the muffled oarlocks, too."

"I noticed them right away," answered Meg. "And, as I started to say, before I was interrupted," she said teasingly, "Jock Cameron wouldn't use a boat with muffled oarlocks, unless he and some of the men have been going night fishing in the quiet water of the bay outside this cave. It's an old fisherman's trick to muffle the oarlocks, especially for night fishing, so as not to make any noise and frighten the fish away."

"But isn't it unusual for fishermen to be using your private bay and beach, Meg?" Cherry asked. "You said they did *sometimes*, but . . ."

Meg now interrupted Cherry with, "It seems they must be using it pretty regularly. Yes, it is unusual. But if Old Jock and some of his friends are concerned, I don't want to say anything. I just wouldn't feel right about it. All the same, it might be a good idea to find out just what is going on around here."

As they talked, the girls had been picking their way through the passage and down the steps to the ledge along the side of the cave. They now stood at the end of the ledge in the daylight.

"We could ask Lloyd," suggested Cherry. "He might know."

"I doubt it," Meg said. "He doesn't get to hear much about island goings-on. You see, he's been away so long that Balfourians consider him almost an outsider, so they're careful what they say to him. Of course they'll get used to him in time. No, the best way to find out about this"—she pointed to the boat on the sand below the ledge—"is to keep our own eyes and ears open. Especially you, Cherry Ames."

"Why me? I'm definitely an outsider," Cherry pointed out.

"But I think you are more observant than any of us," Meg declared, then added mischievously, "Also, because you have a penchant for solving mysteries, so Dr. Fortune told me."

CHAPTER IX

The Man on the Hill

IN THE WEEKS THAT FOLLOWED THE VISIT TO ROGUES'
Cave, Cherry saw little of either Meg or Lloyd.

Meg had begun working as a volunteer in the office
at the hospital. In addition, she was helping out at
the library in the afternoons until someone could be
found to replace the librarian's young assistant who
had left to get married. Meg spent most evenings until bedtime with her father. She was too busy to be
bothered about rowboats with muffled oars or creels
with initials on them.

Meg was very happy to see her father's day-by-day
improvement. Dr. Mac had taken Sir Ian off the
Sippy diet, and had introduced a diet high in nutri-
tion for him, to which Sir Ian had responded well.
Although Sir Ian was still weak and any unusual effort tired him, both Dr. Mac and Cherry found his
reactions to the change in diet very encouraging.

Lloyd was utterly absorbed in the mines. He practically "ate, drank, and slept" Balfour Mines. However, he always dropped in to see his uncle for a few minutes every day, then hurried back to the Mine Office.

Cherry, left in the great house with Sir Ian and the servants, was not kept as occupied as Meg and Lloyd. With his improving condition, her patient's needs were less. And he made less demands upon her. In fact, he did not want to be helped.

"I often smile to myself," Cherry wrote to the five Spencer Club girls with whom she always shared an apartment when she was in New York City, "because Sir Ian's attitude is just like that of a small boy who is determined to be on his own. The other day he told me quite cockily that he could go downstairs by himself when I tried to guide him as he fumbled with his foot for the next step. Also for two hours in the morning, he has been shutting himself in the library to work. The doctor has warned him that he must take it easy, not overdo. So I tap on the door and call 'Time's up' when two hours have passed. Sir Ian comes out grumbling 'One of these days, nurse lass, ye can tap a hole in the door like a woodpecker and I'll pay ye no mind a-tall.' "

Since her duties were not now so consuming of time and effort, and she was quite often alone, Cherry found her attention kept turning to the boat with the muffled oarlocks and Old Jock Cameron's tote bag —if, indeed, it were his—in the hidey-hole.

From her windows, Cherry could look down over the cliffs. Although she often watched for a rowboat entering or leaving the bay at Rogues' Cave, she

never saw one. She tried to draw out the Barclay servants by asking if they had seen a rowboat in the bay.
None of them had. Ramsay, the gardener, went down
to the beach one day to get sand and pebbles for the
garden walks. When he returned, Cherry asked if he
had noticed a rowboat in the cave.

"The day Miss Meg and I visited the cave, we saw
one," Cherry said.

"Then someone must have taken it away," Ramsay
replied. "I dinna see any boat."

Then one morning while Cherry was having her
"elevenses"—the customary tea at eleven o'clock—an
interesting thing took place. She was sitting in the
sun on the terrace near the kitchen, drinking her tea,
when she became aware of Tess and a man talking
inside.

Cherry heard the man say, "Na, na, Tess, ye
canna persuade me. I'll na go upstairs to see Sir Ian."

"Then why do ye come here every day to pester
me with questions?" Tess asked tartly. "How does he
feel today? ye ask. Is he better? ye ask. What did he
do today? ye ask. Did Sir Ian ask for me and did ye
tell him that Old Jock was only waiting for him to get
weel? ye ask. What's the trouble with you, Jock
Cameron? Ye should go talk with your old friend, Sir
Ian, and find out for yourself."

"I've my reasons," came Old Jock's reply. "Dinna
ask me what they are, for I'll na tell ye. When I'm
ready to see my friend, I'll come and na afore. And
mark ye, Tess, ye are not to tell him or anyone else,
I come here."

"Is he and all Balfour to think, then, ye have forsaken Sir Ian in his sickness, Jock Cameron?" demanded Tess.

"Ah, 'tis something that canna be helped," Old Jock said, and his voice sounded sad.

The back door closed. Cherry stood up to catch a glimpse of him, but shrubbery hid the kitchen entrance and she did not see him as he left.

When, a few minutes later, Tess came out to clear away the tea things, Cherry said, "I'm afraid I heard you talking with Mr. Cameron just now."

Tess looked startled at first, then she said, "But I know ye waudna tell Sir Ian about Old Jock. Even though I get angry with Old Jock and his stubbornness, I trust him to do what he thinks is best for his friend. Ye must not think hard of him, Miss Cherry, for all he is acting so strangely."

Cherry scarcely knew what to think of the man. She did wish that she could get a chance to talk with him herself.

Cherry had made a habit of taking a walk in the afternoon after tea. Usually she went to the top of the hill of the abandoned mine, for there was a glorious view of the sea and the island from there.

One sunshiny afternoon, about three weeks after her arrival on Balfour, Cherry started out on her usual afternoon walk.

She was at the foot of the hill when she saw the top of a man's head appear just above the crest. He was walking up the other side and appeared bit by bit—head, shoulders, arms, body—as though he were a seed shown sprouting by delayed photography. As soon as he reached the summit of the hill, he looked about on all sides. Cherry, standing behind a scrubby black oak, escaped his attention.

Evidently satisfied that he was not observed, the man took something from his coat pocket and a second later Cherry saw a bright flash. He repeated the flash several times, turning in his hand what she decided was a mirror, to reflect the sun.

All the while he flashed his mirror, the man was gazing intently at something beyond the cliffs, not too far from shore.

For ten or more minutes, she watched him signaling with his mirror the dots and dashes of the Morse code. It seemed to her a curious thing for the man to be doing. She wished she could have read the message he was sending with his short and long flashes. Then, even as she was watching, the man vanished. She saw him bending over among the bushes one moment, and the next, he was gone.

Cherry started running up the hill, fully expecting to see the man reappear at any instant. She reached the summit, however, without any sign of him. A quick glance down the opposite side revealed that he had not gone in that direction. The hillsides were empty of movement, except for the scurry of a rabbit or other small animal among the rocks and bushes. Cherry leaned against the big rock, which was at the very peak of the hill in the stiff grass and bushes, to catch her breath.

It came to her after a while where she had seen the man before. He was the short, muscular man, in the sharply tailored dark clothes, who had jostled her the day she and the Barclays had come over on the

Sandy Fergus. She had had a good look at him on the boat. With the sun shining on him up there on the hill, she had seen him clearly.

Wondering to whom the man had been signaling, she scrambled up on the rock for a better view of the sea. She felt the rock tilt as if it were loose in its socket of earth. It was an odd sort of rock—gray and peculiarly rough and pitted, rather like foam.

Getting her balance, Cherry stood up on the rock and peered eagerly beyond the cliffs. She observed a fishing schooner a little way out from shore and a large rowboat coming toward the island. It was headed, so she thought, in the direction of the Barclays' private beach.

The boat was coming on and she saw that there were half a dozen or more men in it, four of whom were straining at the oars evidently in an effort to increase its speed. As they drew closer, Cherry perceived that they were maneuvering the boat to head it into the pass between the rocks at the entrance to the little bay at Rogues' Cave.

"The tide!" Cherry cried aloud. "When the tide is in . . ." It dawned on her then what Meg had meant about sailing the ketch when she and Lloyd were kids. They had had to wait for the tide, in order to get in and out of the bay.

Now Cherry knew why the man had been signaling. He was letting the men in the fishing schooner know when it was safe to come in with the rowboat. That was it, Cherry decided.

The men guided the boat through the pass between

the rocks and were lost to view under the brow of the cliff above Rogues' Cave.

She continued to watch, and presently the rowboat reappeared. It was loaded with some sort of cargo in sacks, which must have been heavy, for the boat was low in the water and the men were rowing with great effort. Upon reaching the fishing schooner, the sacks of whatever it was they contained, were put aboard, the men followed, then the rowboat was hauled up and stowed on deck. The fishing schooner sailed away to the south toward St. John's.

Cherry started back down the hill, her mind busy with what she had just seen.

Within a short distance of the house, someone sang out gaily, "Hi, beautiful! How about a lift?"

And there was Lloyd, driving along the road in one of the company's "Bugs," as he called the little two-seater cars which were used by the various department heads of the mines to get about on the island.

Cherry walked over to the car. "Hello, Lloyd. I'd be glad of a lift. I've been up and down that big hill," she said, getting in.

"What were you doing, training for the next expedition to the top of Mount Everest?" he teased, reaching over and tugging a curl. "You look to be in fine condition for it, Miss Ames. Your cheeks are rosy red and your hair is fair glorious."

"Now, none of your flattery, Mr. Barclay," Cherry said. "I want you to be serious. I've something important to tell you."

"I'm all ears," he replied, grinning at her. Then, frowning exaggeratedly, he said, "Speak, fair lady."

"Oh, do be serious," Cherry said, smiling in spite of herself. "A very strange thing happened on the hill this afternoon. I met . . ."

"Ah, poor lass," interrupted Lloyd, shaking his head sadly. "Ye must have run into Rorie Gill. He's often on the hill."

"I wish you had told me," said Cherry tartly.

As though he had not heard her, Lloyd went on dolefully, with more head shaking, "Rorie Gill. I waudna have thought it. Usually you see him in the fall when the Hunter's Moon is rising over the Balfour hills and crags." His voice began to roll dramatically, as Lloyd continued, "Rorie rides by moonlight on his dark horse and mounts to the crest of the hill. There he sits, peering out to sea until he sights a rich-laden ship approaching Balfour Harbor. Then Rorie rides down again, and, with the hollow laughing cry of the loon, summons his merrymen around him."

Cherry laughed. "Lloyd Barclay, you are a much worse tease than my brother Charlie," she accused him. "Please be serious for a moment."

"Na, na, Cherry lass, I'm no in the mood now," he told her. "It's not Uncle Ian or ye waudna be on the hill. So . . ." He shrugged.

"Well, what makes you so gay this afternoon?" demanded Cherry. "And why are you coming home from the mines so early and as lightheaded and merry as a chipmunk?"

"I'll not tell you until you've had your say," Lloyd

replied with a self-righteous air. "You're bursting to talk, so out with it."

They had reached the house and Lloyd drove up in front and stopped. "Let's just sit here in the Bug," he said.

Cherry poured out everything in a rush, keeping back only the part about Jock Cameron. When she finished, Lloyd laughed heartily at her and said, "Cherry, this island is a great place to stimulate the imagination. You go ahead and be as fanciful as you like. But the facts are that there are good fishing grounds just beyond the rocks at Rogues' Cave. In the old days, the Barclays reserved them for themselves. The fishermen have always respected the rights, I suppose you'd call them. And off-islanders have left Balfour waters to the Balfourians for the most part. But times have changed.

"That fishing schooner you saw," Lloyd went on to explain, "may belong to some off-islander. Those sacks could have been filled with sand to be used for ballast in the schooner. Might even have been rocks. They're both used for ballast. Of course I don't want fishermen using our bay and beach and making a nuisance of themselves." He paused, thought a moment, then asked, "Would you describe the man again that you saw on the hill?"

Cherry repeated the description she had given him of the short, muscular man. "I saw him once before," she told Lloyd. "He was on the *Sandy Fergus* the day we came to Balfour."

"You know, Cherry, that must be Joseph Tweed, 'Little Joe' as he is called," Lloyd said, his expression becoming stern. "He was hanging around outside the Mine Office last week. Someone pointed him out to me and said that Little Joe had been seen a number of times, talking to miners from Number 2 mine. I think you probably saw Little Joe again today. I can't think why he's hanging around the island. Five or six years ago, Little Joe worked as a foreman in Number 2 mine. Then it was discovered that he was doing business as a loan shark on the side. If a miner had to borrow twenty-five or thirty dollars in a hurry, he would go to Little Joe and get it at once without any bankers' formalities. Of course Little Joe charged about fifty cents interest on every dollar borrowed, and he wanted his money and interest back in a week or two. When Uncle Ian found this out, he fired Little Joe. He could have had the man arrested, but Uncle Ian let him off with a warning. Little Joe went to St. John's and from all reports has done extremely well—owns property, a boat or two, has an interest in several businesses. He's what is known in the States as a very smart operator and his reputation is none too good."

"What do you suppose he *is* doing on the island?" asked Cherry.

"That's what I'd like to know," Lloyd replied. "I'm glad you told me all this, Cherry. Now I'll be on the lookout. See if Little Joe is up to something."

"I think I'd better go in," Cherry said. "It's getting late."

Lloyd opened the car door and she got out.

"Oh, by the way," he said, "the entrance to the old mine shaft is on the top of the hill. Last time I was up there years ago, the opening was covered with boards and all grown over with vines and bushes. I don't suppose you noticed it."

"No, I didn't," answered Cherry. "There's a big rock sitting right on top of the hill."

"And I expect it was just a-sittin' still, like the one in the verse that begins 'I wish I was a little rock,'" Lloyd said with a big grin.

"And ends 'Doin' nothin' all day long, but just a-sittin' still,'" Cherry quoted at random, returning his grin. She started to go, then stopped. "By the way, you were going to tell me what put you in such a gay, carefree mood today, Mr. Barclay."

"Tell you and Meg both at dinner," he said.

At dinner that evening Lloyd reported to Cherry and Meg that the work in the new mine was going by leaps and bounds under McGuire's supervision. The ore was very high assay, a much greater yield of iron than had been anticipated. Things were not going badly, either, at old Number 2, under Jock Cameron.

"I believe Balfour Mines may even make a profit this year if we can only keep it up," Lloyd declared.

"I hope so. Oh, I hope so," said Meg earnestly.

"Under the eagle eye of Mining Engineer Lloyd Barclay, I say they will," Cherry declared grandly.

~~~~~~

CHAPTER X

A Meeting in St. John's

SIR IAN HAD CONTINUED TO FEEL BETTER AND RE-
spond well to the diet of bland foods which Dr. Mac
had prescribed. Under Cherry's direction, Tess, the
cook, carefully prepared the small, frequent meals
and took great pride in doing so.

"But he'll no get well entirely with all the proper
food in the world," Tess predicted. "He's sore trou-
bled in his mind. Sir Ian has to put up with the wild
spending of his brother and sister in England. And
the mines, too, na weel for so long. His fine, helpful
brother, who was Master Lloyd's father, died, and
left Sir Ian to carry the whole burden of the Barclays.
'Tis muckle burden for one man."

Yet, in spite of his big burden, Sir Ian was recov-
ering little by little under Cherry's capable nursing
care. No small part was due to Lloyd, who was slowly
making his uncle realize that here was someone who
was a true Barclay, worthy to take over the Balfour

Mines someday. Bit by bit, Sir Ian's mind was being relieved about the operation of the mines.

It was during the fifth week that Cherry had been at Barclay House that Sir Ian began to walk about in the garden. He expressed a longing to take a ride in the car. Dr. Mac thought it a good idea. So on the following Sunday afternoon, Lloyd suggested that his uncle and Cherry go for a drive with him since it was the chauffeur's Sunday off. Meg was going to the hospital with the doctor to help him catch up with some more paper work in the office.

"Da, we need a good hospital and proper professional assistance," Meg said. "Douglas is working himself to the bone with all he has to do. And I don't want to marry a bag of bones."

"I'd give him his hospital now if there was the money for it," her father said.

"Oh, Da dear, you talk like a feudal baron or something, making a gift to his retainers," Meg told him. "The community has a *right* to an adequate hospital with adequate medical staff. This isn't the Middle Ages, Da, you old darling." She gave him a resounding kiss on the top of his head as he sat in the hall downstairs, waiting for Lloyd to bring the car around.

Meg had started outside when Sir Ian called after her, "What's this about marrying that sandy-haired pill pusher? Has he asked ye yet?"

"No, but he will," Meg answered merrily. "Only a matter of time now." She paused, then added, "Oh, dear, I do hope Bess Cowan doesn't make any of those dreary remarks of hers about the 'turrible responsibilities of the wedded state' before Douglas. I do wish someone cheerier were on duty today at the hospital."

Meg darted out the door, looking like a butterfly in her yellow dress, and into her car.

A few minutes later Lloyd brought his car and Sir Ian settled himself comfortably in the back seat, while Cherry sat in front beside Lloyd.

There was a good paved road that followed the shore almost all the way around the island. Lloyd drove through the village with its little frame cottages, scattered along the narrow streets winding up the hillsides or curving along the waterfront.

They came to the hospital and Lloyd said, "Meg has been saying 'We must take Cherry to see the hospital, I'm sure she'd like to visit it.' But it was just one of those things we didn't get around to doing. So I told myself that today's the day Miss Ames visits our local hospital. How about it, Cherry?"

"Of course I'd love it," she said. "Do you mind, Sir Ian?"

"Not at all. Not at all," he replied.

Lloyd turned the car off the road and into the drive that led to the back of the one-story, white frame building. He stopped in the parking space there.

The hospital faced the road with its back to the bay. Cherry looked beyond the sandy beach to where it seemed countless small boats with white sails were skimming over the blue waters of Balmaghie Bay.

Meg came running out the rear entrance of the building. "Hello, everybody!" she called.

"Cherry, you and Lloyd go with Meg to see the hospital," Sir Ian said. "I'm going to sit here in the car and enjoy watching the sailboats."

"Dr. Mac can show them around," Meg said, laughing and getting into the car.

Lloyd and Cherry went inside. A central hall ran through the building from front to back. The various rooms opened off this hall down which Dr. Mac was striding toward them.

"Well, isn't this a nice surprise!" he cried.

"I've brought Miss Ames to see Balfour Hospital," announced Lloyd with exaggerated formality. "We want the dollar tour."

"That's the Mackenzie Special," replied the doctor with equal formality. "Right this way, folks!"

It did not take the doctor long to show them around the hospital. It was quite small—too small as Meg had pointed out to her father, to serve adequately the island's population. There was no operating room, so patients in need of a serious operation had to go to St. John's. The hospital needed more of everything from beds to laboratory equipment, but Cherry was impressed with how light, airy, and sparklingly clean the place was. It had the appearance of being well managed. And as Bess Cowan, the tall, gray-haired nurse, said as Cherry and Lloyd were leaving, "It's thanks to Dr. Mackenzie that we can do so much with so little. Do you know, Miss Ames, this hospital is considered above average in quality of service, in spite of its inadequacies, because of him!"

"Mac and I will see you at dinner," Meg called after the car, as Cherry, Lloyd, and Sir Ian went around the drive and onto the road toward the mines.

They passed the mines, stopping at one of them so Cherry could see the entrance shaft with its elevator to take the miners deep under the ground, and she had a look at some of the adits or exits from which the ore was brought by cars or conveyor systems.

Lloyd kept pointing out what must be done about better facilities and new equipment. Only the new mine received Lloyd's unqualified approval.

"You really did yourself proud, Uncle Ian, on that new mine," Lloyd told him. "The best and most modern pumps, conveyors, elevators, power drills—the works. It must have cost you a small fortune."

"It did," Sir Ian said grimly.

The road continued to Carse Point at the extreme north end of the island where the lighthouse stood, and there was a lifesaving station, and a Coast Guard cutter riding at anchor off shore.

The road left Carse Point and ran now along the ocean side of the island, with beaches and coves, then climbed up to the cliffs.

After a while, the road left the cliffs and turned across the island, winding through hills, dales, and woods until it brought them back to Barclay House.

It was a delightful drive and all three of them enjoyed it immensely. Sir Ian appeared refreshed by it and not tired at all. That evening Sir Ian joined Lloyd and Meg in the library where Higgins, the butler, had laid a small fire in the fireplace. On Balfour, even in summer, the nights were cool.

Cherry took the opportunity to catch up on her correspondence, which she had not found time to do that week. She had kept her mother and father up to date with events on the island, so they knew about Rogues' Cave and the happenings on the hill of the abandoned mine. She wound up the letter with a description of the day's trip around the island.

On Tuesday, Cherry had a day off and planned a shopping trip to St. John's. She liked walking and she needed another suitable pair of shoes. Her one pair had become quite worn from her daily walks on the rocky island. She could not find what she wanted in the little village store, so there was nothing to do but try the stores in St. John's.

She did not have to worry about Sir Ian, for Meg was going to take care of her father.

"I'll take you to the ferry when I go to work," Lloyd told Cherry. "Then I'll meet you when it returns this afternoon, and I'll bring you back here."

So it was all settled when Cherry, Meg, and Lloyd went down to breakfast a few minutes past eight o'clock Tuesday morning.

They drank their fruit juice. Then, Norah, the maid, brought in a plate of poached eggs to place with the cereal and other dishes on the buffet.

Lloyd was lifting eggs onto his plate when Higgins came in to say there was a call for him.

"I'll take it in the library," Lloyd said.

A few moments later Cherry and Meg heard him shouting into the phone: "What do you mean the pump won't suck? . . . Of course that pump hasn't enough suction. Get the big power pump. . . . Oh! McGuire's using it in the new mine. Never mind. . . . Never mind, I said. I'll be right down."

Lloyd slammed down the receiver. Coming to the dining-room door, he informed Cherry and Meg that he had to rush down to the mines.

"A leak has been found in one of the chambers of Number 2 mine," he told them. "It's a chamber nearest the abandoned mine, and it's flooded. Cameron left word at the office that he would be in St. John's on business. McGuire has his hands full with the new mine. I've got to go down myself."

Lloyd gulped some coffee and hurried into the hall, calling back over his shoulder, "I'm terribly sorry, Cherry, not to take you to the ferry. Please forgive me. Meg, look after Cherry, will you?" And he went outside and drove off in the Bug.

After Lloyd left, Cherry told Meg how much she had enjoyed the drive around the island the Sunday before because she had been thinking ever since that she had never known a place so filled with beauty and legends. From talking about the island, the two drifted into talk about Rogues' Cave.

And Meg said, "Higgins knows all the old tales and he used to tell me stories by the hour. I suppose he told you how my grandda, when he was a boy, was lost in the cave."

"Oh, yes," Cherry said. "And he said your grandfather used to do experiments in the room at the top of the tower and that he wrote in his secret journal by the light of a candle at night."

"That's right!" exclaimed Meg. "When I was a little girl, I used to go up there, thinking I'd look for the secret journal. But I was much more interested in peering out through the telescope than in anything else." She paused, then went on eagerly. "You know what, Cherry!"

"No, what?" replied Cherry, grinning.

"Let's go up to the tower sometime and search together. We might even get Lloyd to go with us." Meg stopped and considered that. "Oh, he wouldn't go," she decided. "He'd probably think it too childish for anything. But, Cherry, you're in the house a lot. When you have a free hour or so, why don't you go up to the tower room and look for Grandda's secret journal yourself?"

Cherry's eyes sparkled. "Now, I think that would be fun!" she exclaimed. "A secret journal. A room in a tower. That's an exciting combination."

Meg laughed gaily. "If you do decide to go when I'm not here," she said, "look behind the tapestry that covers the end of the hall on the second floor. You'll see an old ironwork door. Go through it and climb the stairs until you reach the very top of the tower."

Meg looked at the clock on the wall above the dining-room fireplace. "Oh, dear!" she cried out. "Cherry, I have to beg off taking you to the ferry. I promised Ramsay I'd see him first thing this morning and tell him where to plant the new shrubs. And if I know Ramsay, he's champing at the bit this very minute. Smith will take you, Cherry. I'll tell him right away. I'd better run. Please excuse me, Cherry."

Meg pushed her chair back, and going out the French windows that opened onto the dining terrace, ran down the path toward the gardener's stone cottage at the west end of the grounds.

Presently, Higgins came to tell Cherry that Smith was ready with the car any time she wanted to leave.

Dressed in a pretty woolen skirt, bright cashmere sweater and cardigan, with a close-fitting hat to keep

her curls in place in the wind, Cherry stuck her head
in Sir Ian's room to tell him she was leaving.

"Have a good time shopping, for I know ye are no
different from Meg when it comes to that," he said.
"And don't take it amiss if the lads stare at ye," he
added. "They waudna be able to help themselves. Ye
are as pretty as the morning, Cherry lass."

"Ah, thank ye, Sir Ian," Cherry told him with an
impish grin at mimicking his accent. "As your daughter says, ye've a silver tongue with compliments."

It was a beautiful morning. The sky was bright
with the sun. Overhead the scattered clouds were
floating lazily.

When she got out of the car at the wharf, Captain
Rab was just going aboard the *Sandy Fergus*. He rec-
ognized her at once and they exchanged greetings.
Then he invited her into the wheelhouse.

"Meg always cons the helm, that is, watches the
course while I steer," he told her with a chuckle,
"whenever she makes a trip to St. John's."

Cherry settled herself on the window seat and
she and the captain talked about the Barclays and
how much she was enjoying her stay on Balfour.

It lacked some minutes of time for departure and
there were not many passengers on the boat as yet.
Cherry noticed a passenger leaning over the rail.
With a start she recognized the man that she had
seen on the hill.

"Who is that?" she asked Captain Rab, pointing
the man out.

"Oh, that's Joseph Tweed," replied Captain Rab.
"He's known as 'Little Joe' Tweed. Lives in St.

John's. He promotes prize fights, speculates in stocks, owns a fishing schooner called the *Heron*. Always seems to have money. I dinna like the man."

Cherry told Captain Rab then about seeing Little Joe on the hill.

"Peering out at his fishing schooner, ye say," said the captain. "He's a wise man to keep an eye on her. A rougher lot of men I've not seen in many a day as Little Joe has for a crew. And the captain's no better. He's had his license suspended too often for any respectable ship owner to hire him."

It was time to start. The captain clanged the bell and shouted to a deck hand to cast off the mooring lines. The engine roared into action and the boat got under way.

On the way to St. John's, Captain Rab observed the steady fall of the barometer and remarked that he "dinna" like it. "There's dirty weather knocking about," he told Cherry, pulling at his pipe.

The crossing was choppy and the sky was becoming feathered with clouds when the *Sandy Fergus* reached the St. John's wharf.

"Ye had best take the May Bee going back," the captain advised Cherry. "She leaves earlier and will make it over to the island afore this storm breaks. Of course if ye dinna mind a bit of wind and water, the *Sandy Fergus* leaves around four o'clock. I'd be happy to have the pleasure of your company."

Cherry thanked him and told him that it depended upon how long it took her to do her shopping whether she would go back on the helicopter or the boat.

At a quarter past two she had finished her shopping. She had even taken a little time to have lunch, buy postcards, and send them with brief notes to Dr. Joe, the Spencer Club girls, Midge, Ruth Dale, and other friends at Hilton Hospital, as well as to her family.

The sky was overcast by two o'clock. Inquiries about the May Bee revealed that it would not be taking off since a storm was coming up. It began to rain. There was nothing to do but wait for the *Sandy Fergus*.

Cherry, with a full shopping bag and a couple of packages which she could not cram into it, dodged into a pleasant-looking coffee shop near the wharf. She sat down at a table beside a window which faced the harbor, and ordered chocolate milk and cookies. The waitress told her the ferryboat came in around three or shortly thereafter.

Cherry glanced around the restaurant at a number of well-dressed women and children, a few girls, and several businessmen.

One man at a table in a corner drew her attention by his frequent glances toward the entrance and then at his wrist watch to check the time. Obviously he was expecting someone who was late. He did not appear to be a man accustomed to waiting. There was an air of importance about him. He was well groomed and wore finely tailored clothes. His hair was a distinguished salt and pepper, but his eyes and mouth were hard, and the whole cast of the face was that of a man of authority.

Cherry watched his growing annoyance for a while, then gazed outside. It had grown prematurely

Obviously the man was expecting someone

dark. Lights began to appear along the waterfront and on the craft in the harbor. The wind steadily increased and rain now bounced off the street.

There was a boat moored to the wharf a few yards away. Cherry read the name *Heron,* lettered on the side.

"So that's Joseph—Little Joe—Tweed's fishing schooner," she thought. Just as she was about to turn away, she saw a man coming up the wharf. He stopped under the light to look at the *Heron,* as though to be sure it was the right vessel, then jumped lightly aboard.

That moment was time enough for Cherry to recognize Jock Cameron.

"Can it be possible that Old Jock and Little Joe Tweed are connected in some way?" she asked herself.

While she was thinking this over, the door of the coffee shop opened and two men entered, slapping their wet hats against glistening raincoats.

Cherry gasped. They were the pilot Jerry Ives and Little Joe Tweed!

"There's Mr. Broderick over there," said Little Joe, loudly enough for everyone in the restaurant to hear.

The two walked directly to the table in the corner. Mr. Broderick appeared extremely annoyed. Little Joe started to say something, but Broderick would not let him finish. He rose, put on his coat, picked up his hat, and motioning for Jerry Ives to follow him, strode out of the coffee shop.

Little Joe watched them leave, then left the shop himself and, walking to the *Heron,* went aboard.

CHAPTER XI

The Storm

THE WAITRESS HAD TOLD CHERRY TO WATCH OUT THE window for the arrival of the ferryboat.

"You'll see a bright light with 'Ferry' on it up over the wharf where Captain Rab always moors. He switches it on as soon as he comes in."

At ten minutes to three Cherry saw the *Heron* leave the wharf and head north in the direction of Balfour Island.

At five minutes to three the sign "Ferry" lighted up. Gathering her shopping bag and parcels, Cherry tore out of the restaurant and down the wharf.

"Ah, there ye are," Captain Rab said, helping her aboard. "I was hoping ye would be along to con the helm for me on the way back." He directed her toward the wheelhouse, telling her, "There'll no be many on this trip, so we'll be pushing off soon."

Within half an hour five passengers sprinted aboard and ducked into the cabin like homing pigeons. At twenty minutes to four, when no more passengers showed up, Captain Rab set out.

Cherry was to remember for a long time the rough passage from St. John's to Balfour Harbor. Certainly she had never seen so much sea so close before. The *Sandy Fergus* plunged and wallowed and rolled. Cherry looked out the wheelhouse window and they seemed to be hedged in by waves that broke frothing over the bows.

"Told ye we'd catch it," remarked Captain Rab. "Said so this morning before it came over the radio."

"We seem to be in the middle of the storm," said Cherry.

"Oh, no," the captain answered. "We're sailing ahead of it. She's coming up the coast instead of blowing out to sea as the weatherman predicted earlier. Favoring us with a taste of foul weather."

To all outward appearance, Captain Rab was not particularly concerned. He concentrated on the sea ahead and steered the vessel. There were marker buoys to indicate the channel and whistling buoys crying a "Whoo-Whoo" warning to stay away from rocks and reefs.

The rain fell harder and the wind rose. The gleam of the boat's lights caught the flight of the spray. Lightning flickered and thunder rumbled off in the distance.

Inside the wheelhouse the radio blurted, predicting the course of the storm, reporting damage left in her wake, warning boats and ships to get out of the track of the high wind, telling of ships in danger, distress, or believed lost.

The spell of the storm had fallen upon Cherry. She was absorbed by it. For a while, she gave all her attention to the angry waters, the noise, and the rolling boat. Once she spoke to ask if Captain Rab knew a Mr. James Broderick.

"Know him by sight and reputation," the captain answered. "Snatches companies the way a jaeger snatches fish from gulls and terns."

Shutting out the storm, she gave herself over to her thoughts. The experience in the coffee shop had been puzzling. What did Old Jock, Little Joe Tweed, Jerry Ives, and James Broderick have to do with each other? Cherry asked herself. "They probably don't have any connection at all," she chided herself. "I'm letting my imagination run away with itself. It doesn't seem likely that Old Jock and Tweed could have any mutual interests. Of course Old Jock did go aboard Little Joe's boat. I wonder why he did that?"

Cherry was startled by a sudden pitch of the boat that almost tossed her off the window bench on which she was sitting. Captain Rab grunted and swung the helm to head the boat again into the wind.

Cherry felt a shiver of fear as the *Sandy Fergus* labored on against the wind, shaken by the waves, and creaking in all her timbers. The calm face and unruffled manner of Captain Rab was wonderfully reassuring, however, and she pushed her fear aside.

Before long the waves became less violent and Cherry could make out the shape of the bay at Balfour Island. When they entered the harbor, she realized the waters seemed less wild only in relation to those through which they had just passed. The waves were rolling in enormous swells and pounding upon the beach.

With difficulty, Captain Rab brought the ferryboat alongside the wharf and got her safely moored. The five passengers scuttled ashore.

"There's Smith come to fetch ye," the captain said to Cherry.

Cherry looked where he pointed and saw the Barclay chauffeur, with head bent to the wind, running toward them.

Smith took her bag and bundles and gave her a raincoat which she drew over her head and about her like a shawl. She called good-by to Captain Rab and ran with Smith to the car.

Settled inside the Rolls-Royce, Cherry looked out on the empty streets. People had shut themselves indoors and the village appeared deserted. The harbor was filled with vessels straining at their moorings, but she did not see the *Heron* among them.

At Barclay House she found Sir Ian the only member of the family at home. Meg was at the hospital, for there had already been several casualties and she had gone to help the doctor and Bess Cowan, the nurse. Lloyd was still at the mines.

When Higgins let Cherry in, Sir Ian called out to her from the drawing room.

"That ye, Cherry? Ye are just in time for tea."

Cherry joined Sir Ian in front of the window where the tea table had been placed, so he could watch the storm. He had the radio on to get the latest reports on its progress. The storm was expected to reach its greatest force on Balfour sometime that night before it blew out to sea. It had been losing strength as it traveled overland and was averaging about twelve miles an hour. But inhabitants were warned to take every precaution to ensure the safety of life and the protection of property.

Cherry had never seen Sir Ian when he was calmer than he was right then. He was not worried in the least. In fact, she got the feeling that the storm was having a good effect on him, as absurd as that might sound. He drank his tea and spread thin slices of white bread with unsalted butter in complete tranquillity. But his eyes were shining and alert to every nuance of the wind and rain, and the reports over the radio claimed his attention.

"Remove swinging signs from store fronts," the announcer intoned. "Brace sizable glass areas against wind pressure with stout boards. Take in ash cans, furniture from porches and gardens, and other movable objects. They are dangerous hazards when blown about by the gale."

"I was expecting a visitor this evening," Sir Ian said when the announcer had completed the latest news bulletin. "It's not likely he'll arrive for a day or two unless he rides the wind." He heaved a rumbling sigh and continued, "I love a storm. It's a wonderfully dramatic thing, a storm. Man may be dwarfed by a hurricane or a typhoon, but he's also made great by his battle against great odds. Through the night and in the darkness I think of the lighthouse at Carse Point flashing out its beam against the storm. Of how the radio beacons reach out to sea."

Sir Ian sat a while longer with Cherry, watching and enjoying the wild scene outside, then he said, "I think I'm tired, lass. Like to lie down a bit."

With Cherry beside him, he went slowly upstairs.

"Ye needn't be afraid in this house," he told her on the way up. "It's solid as rock. Withstood the tempests for two hundred years. Years ago my father and I liked to sit in the tower with a storm raging all round. From there we could watch the whole splendor of land and sea and sky."

Cherry saw that Sir Ian was comfortable, then went to her own room to put away her purchases and change into her uniform.

"I wonder if the visitor Sir Ian expected was Mr. Broderick," she suddenly thought. "Perhaps Jerry Ives was going to fly his boss over but the storm held them up."

She was disappointed not to have seen Meg and Lloyd to tell them about her trip to St. John's.

At eight o'clock there was a knock on her door. Cherry rushed to open it, expecting to see Meg, but it was Norah, the maid, to tell her that Miss Meg had called to say that neither she nor Lloyd would be home until later.

"I was to explain that they're engaged with The Volunteers," Norah said, "and to tell Tess and Higgins not to hold back dinner for them." The maid shook her head. "I fear this is one of the Wild Ones and sure to cause harm on land and sea."

Cherry interpreted "Wild Ones" as referring to storms, and agreed with Norah heartily that this one undoubtedly was wild. She told Norah that she and

Sir Ian would be down to dinner in a few minutes, and the maid left.

After his rest, Sir Ian was almost chipper during the evening meal. Cherry's mood rose to match his and they were quite gay, laughing and talking.

Sir Ian took as a matter of course Meg's and Lloyd's work with The Volunteers, of whom Norah had spoken earlier.

Sir Ian explained that it was a voluntary organization composed of various groups of men and women who had specific jobs to do in any emergency, such as a fire, storm, or flood. There was a Fire Brigade, an Ambulance Corps and so on, as well as lookouts stationed at intervals along the shore, to aid the coastguardmen who were on duty at Carse Point Lighthouse.

"I regret I canna be with them," Sir Ian told Cherry. " 'Tis the responsibility of a Barclay to be working with the others when there's trouble."

For an hour after dinner, they listened to the news broadcasts. The course of the storm remained unchanged. Before they went upstairs to bed, Norah brought in some candles.

"The electricity is not such a certainty that these may not come in handy," Norah said, giving each of them several large candles.

Sir Ian grinned. "Why, Norah, these are enough to last for days," he said.

"Ye had best keep them," she cautioned. "There's no telling once the lights go off when they'll come on again."

"Norah always expects the worst," Sir Ian said to

Cherry and laughed. "It's her dour Scottish nature to get her pleasure out of looking on the dark side of things."

Cherry could not sleep with all the turmoil outside. The wind clamored around the house and the rain battered at the windows furiously. She doubted that Meg or Lloyd would even get home that night. Since she was so restless, this seemed like a good time to try to find the secret journal by herself. She would go up to the tower.

Just in case Meg did return, and might want to see her, Cherry left a note on Meg's dressing table: "Dear Meg," she wrote, "I took your suggestion and have gone to the tower room to look for the secret journal. Cherry."

Then, fully armed with flashlight, candles, and matches, Cherry went to the east end of the hall. She lifted the tapestry which covered the wall and came at once upon the ironwork door.

Playing her light up and down, she located the switch, flicked it on, and the room beyond the iron lattice door became bright. She could see stairs along the opposite wall, leading upward.

There was an iron-ring handle. Cherry pulled. The door opened and she found herself in a room with slitlike windows. There were lights over the stairs and she mounted them briskly. She reached the next room above, which was on a level with the third floor of the house. The staircase continued upward to another room.

Now came the spiral staircase to the tower. It had narrow steps winding up to a door.

Keeping close to the wall, Cherry climbed the circular stairs, by the light of a chandelier in the ceiling over the stair well. The switch which she had turned on beside the ironwork door on the second floor of the house, evidently controlled all the lights, although she did notice other switches at the foot of each set of stairs.

At last, she stood before the heavy oak door at the top of the tower. She turned the knob and the door swung open, with a creak of rusty hinges. Beyond was darkness, except for the patch of light in front of the doorway and flashes of lightning, which brightened for an instant the tower room.

With the wind driving the rain against the windows, which were high and wide, and the thunder crashing, the place was altogether eerie. Cherry hesitated before stepping inside, as a chill of fear seemed to envelop her.

She shook it off. A flicker of lightning revealed a chandelier hanging from a ceiling beam. Running her hand along the inside wall near the door, Cherry found an electric switch and the place was at once filled with a pale light.

As soon as she crossed the threshold, she felt as if she had entered the long-ago past. The only modern note in the place was the electric light. Otherwise, the room looked as though it had been lifted out of an ancient castle. Three of the walls of the large, square room were paneled with oak. A stone fireplace almost filled the fourth wall and over the mantel carved in the stone were the crest of the Barclays and the legend:

"All nature hath a tongue. E'en the stones do speak if ye have ears to hear."

There were chairs with high backs, armchairs of wood and leather flanking the hearth, tables of dark wood, and shelves filled with books. A cupboard was set into one wall, and an enormous desk, scarred and stained, had a long, high top composed of little square drawers like a spice cabinet or the shelves of an old apothecary shop.

There were endless objects for her to admire as she walked about: bronze busts of Socrates and several early Greek philosophers—Thales, Heraclitus, Democritus—with badly tarnished name plates. There was a little statue of a rugged horse whose name plate read: "Sawny Bean, our Galloway nag."

But most amazing of all were the rocks. Scattered everywhere about on the surfaces of tables, tops of shelves, the deep sills of the tall windows were rocks of all shapes, sizes, and colors.

Cherry turned her attention to the fireplace. In the huge cavern was a tiny little furnace and oven, such as an earlier chemist might have used for melting metals and other chemical "cooking." The flagstone hearth was discolored and roughened from his experiments.

Poking about among the many fascinating objects, Cherry had almost forgotten why she was up in the tower. She had to have some method of search if she expected to find whether or not the secret journal was there.

"I'll start with the desk," she thought, "and work my way around the room."

On the table silver candelabra, now tarnished black, held tall, dusty candles. The chandelier overhead was the only electric light apparently, and from the high ceiling its glow was too faint to work by. She got out her matches and started to walk to the table to light the candelabra when the electric lights began to flicker and then went out. The lines were down or there had been a failure at the power plant. In any event, Norah's warning had been timely and Cherry was grateful to have plenty of matches and candles.

For a moment she was in complete darkness. Not even a flash of lightning etched the blackness of the tower room. The storm outside raged boisterously, but in a momentary lull, she heard the whispering shuffle of footsteps on the stairs.

There was something odd about the steps which made her think they belonged to neither Meg nor Lloyd. The person on the spiral stairway, climbing up, would appear at any minute. She became icy cold with unreasonable fear.

Her eye caught a glimmer of light outside the door.

"Who's there?" Cherry demanded sharply.

Suddenly a small, dark figure in seaman's oilskins, with a flickering candle held high in one hand, stood in the doorway. Wet glistened on his black slicker and his sou'wester. In his other hand, he carried a bundle wrapped in tarpaulin.

"Who are you?" Cherry asked, with a breath of relief.

"It's only me, Tammie," replied the boy. "Tammie Cameron."

CHAPTER XII

The Secret in the Tower

THE LUSTROUS GLEAM OF THE CANDLES, WHICH Cherry had lighted in the candelabra, brightened the room. Tammie placidly took off his sou'wester and slicker after shaking the water off on the hearth. Then he deposited them, together with his tarpaulin-wrapped bundle, on the deep window sill nearest him. With a plop he sank into one of the armchairs near the hearth, brushed a lock of hair out of his eyes, and regarded Cherry gravely.

"Ye are Miss Ames, Sir Ian's nurse," he said after a minute.

Cherry had a good look now at the boy who had entered the tower room so calmly and made himself quite at home. He was the most self-possessed young person she had seen in a long time. She saw that he was a scrawny, towheaded boy of ten or eleven with a wind-burned face. He had a quaint, old-fashioned air about him that reminded her of a wise, little old man.

"How did you get here in the storm and at this time of night?" asked Cherry.

"I hid in the greenhouse first," he began. "Then I hid on the kitchen stoop until everything was quiet. Then I sneaked into the house and up the stairs and through the iron door at the end of the hall, the way Miss Meg used to take some of us boys and girls to the tower. Then I went down and unlocked the outside door so my grandda can get in. And then I came up here to wait for my grandda. I brought some victuals in case he was hungry." Tammie pointed to the bundle on the window sill.

"You mean your grandfather, Mr. Jock Cameron, is coming here to the tower?" cried Cherry. "What is he coming here *for?*"

"To give me a message for my grandma," answered Tammie.

Cherry went over to the armchair on the other side of the hearth and sat down. "Look, Tammie," she said. "Let's begin at the beginning. Tell me what this is all about."

"I dinna know if I should," replied Tammie. "Grandda made it plain I was to keep my tongue quiet and slip up to the tower without being seen."

"But I've seen you," Cherry pointed out. "Furthermore, when I was in St. John's today, I saw your grandfather go aboard Mr. Joseph Tweed's fishing boat, the *Heron.*"

Tammie's eyes dropped while he considered this. Then, giving her a sidelong glance from beneath lowered lids, he said with a sigh, "Ye must know then about the Bad Ones."

Cherry shook her head. "No, I don't know about the Bad Ones. Suppose you tell me."

"Ah, weel"—Tammie heaved a sigh, his shoulders slumped dejectedly—"ye may as well know. The Bad Ones are Mr. Tweed, the one they call Little Joe, and the captain and crew of the *Heron*. They are smuggling something out of the Old Mine, and taking it out through Rogues' Cave. Grandda has been trying to find out what it is."

"Does your grandfather have any idea what it might be?" asked Cherry.

"All Grandda said was 'Tammie, 'tis a valuable thing whatever it is,'" replied the boy. "Grandda tried many ways to find out. He went fishing so he could watch the *Heron* to see if a boat brought anything from Rogues' Cave to load on board. But the loading must have been done at night, Grandda said, because he saw a boat only once during the daytime loading heavy sacks aboard the *Heron*. Grandda even stayed sometimes in the hidey-hole in Rogues' Cave to try to catch the Bad Ones red-handed."

"The hidey-hole in Rogues' Cave!" exclaimed Cherry. "Does your grandfather know about that?"

"Ay," Tammie nodded. "'Tis a secret my great-grandda shared with the Old Sir Ian. And my great-grandda told the secret to my grandda."

"And your grandfather still hasn't found out what is being smuggled?" asked Cherry.

Tammie thought a moment. "I *think* he knows," the boy said slowly. "But I dinna think he knows for *sure*. To try to make sure, Grandda went to St. John's to stow away on the *Heron*."

"So that's why your grandfather went aboard the *Heron*," Cherry said. "He was a stowaway. Then he must have known somehow that the *Heron* was coming to Balfour Island."

Tammie nodded. "Ay. Grandda had found out that Little Joe and the captain and crew of the *Heron* were all coming to the island tonight."

"And your grandfather told you to come to the tower to wait for him, is that right, Tammie?"

The boy nodded again. "Ay," he said.

"But if he stowed away, how was your grandfather going to get ashore? And how in the world can he get ashore in this storm?" Cherry asked.

"We will just have to wait, I guess, for Grandda to answer that," Tammie said. He sloughed off his black rubber boots and wriggled back into the chair.

Cherry wisely let Tammie alone. Whatever else he might recall, he would tell in his own good time.

In the meantime, it was best to go ahead with her search for the secret journal. After all, that was what she had come up here for. Besides, the search would be sure to arouse Tammie's curiosity. And she hoped to enlist his help. A boy had hidden the journal and who would be more likely to think of hiding places than another boy?

Although the tower room was seldom used nowadays, as Meg had once told her, the maids swept and dusted it once or twice a year. And there were candles in holders placed conveniently about. Cherry lighted the one on the desk and began to look through the little drawers, which resembled so much an oversize spice cabinet. Each drawer had rocks and minerals in it, she discovered. On these were splotches of white paint on which were lettered "salt crystals," "lead sulfide," "carbon," "pitchblende," and so on. Then there were drawers with what Cherry recognized as man-made, rather boy-made she supposed, nuggets, cubes, pellets, thin sheets, and disks. On each of these was a dab of white paint and a symbol, such as Fe, Cu, Ag, Sn, Pb, Au, and so on. There were, she estimated, between twenty and twenty-five different symbols used, although there were many more pieces. There was, for instance, a drawer full of various size pieces labeled "Fe." These were covered with a reddish dust or coat that rubbed off on her hands.

"Looks just like rust," Cherry remarked aloud.

"It is," a voice said in her ear. "Iron will rust away if ye don't paint it."

There was Tammie beside her, watching interestedly.

"How do you know this is iron?" she asked, holding up one of the pieces.

"Because I know iron when I see it," he answered. "Besides it says so on the label." He touched the painted spot with a finger. "Fe. That's short for *ferrum,* iron." Tammie pronounced the Latin word with a strong burr of the r's.

"Then you must know what all these other letters on the rocks and minerals mean," Cherry said.

"Maybe not all for sure," he said modestly. "But almost all. My da and my grandda taught me." Touching the labels, he recited, "Cu, that's copper. Pb, lead. Sn, tin. This little piece with Au, that's gold."

"You really do know," Cherry commented. "Do you live here on the island with your mother and father?" she asked, by way of starting a conversation.

"No, ma'am. My da is a metallurgist. He works for the Canadian government," he said proudly. "He and my mother are up in Labrador. I am staying with Grandma and Grandda until they get settled."

Tammie walked around to the other side of the desk and began fumbling about in one of the drawers, picking up bits of metals and minerals and examining them. He held up a tiny black disk. "This is siller," he announced. "See the label says Ag."

"So that's silver," Cherry said, taking the disk and looking at it. "I don't see any other pieces with Ag on them. But there seems to be quite a lot of iron."

"Oh, it's no hard to find iron on Balfour," said Tammie. He thought a moment. "Nor yet ore with lead in it. But siller now, that's another thing. I wonder where he got it."

"He? Do you mean Old Sir Ian?" asked Cherry. "The father of the Sir Ian we know?"

"The very same," replied Tammie, nodding. "When some of Grandda's friends, like Mr. Morgan, come to visit, they sometimes talk about Old Sir Ian and how their fathers always said that he was a clever boy. He called this his laboratory."

Cherry could feel her excitement mounting, as she asked, "Did you know that Old Sir Ian kept a secret journal?"

Tammie looked at her blankly.

"You know," she explained, "when Old Sir Ian was a boy, he kept a notebook in which he put down what happened each day. He also wrote down his formulas for testing the rocks and minerals."

Tammie's face lighted up. "Oh, you mean like a chemistry notebook."

"Yes, yes," Cherry said quickly. "That's right. Do you know about it?"

Tammie considered the question, pursing his lips and frowning in thought. "Ay, ay, I have heard that Old Sir Ian kept a notebook." He paused, then added brightly, "Are ye searching for it?"

Cherry nodded vigorously. "I simply must find it. Will you help me?"

Tammie was delighted. To hunt for a secret hiding place was fascinating. "If he used a notebook to set down his experiments, it would have to be handy," the boy suggested.

"But if you didn't want anyone to know about it and wanted to keep your experiments secret, where would you put it?" urged Cherry.

Tammie grinned up at Cherry, like a conspirator taking her into his confidence. "I'd keep it handy and hide it too," he said. "Because I might have to put it away quickly if anyone came."

Then he began walking about the fireplace and the desk, sizing everything up as though he were a cat measuring the distance to spring somewhere.

Cherry stood and watched him.

Tammie considered the desk. "Na, not there." He moved to the cupboard and threw open the doors. Shelves were filled with glass tubes, beakers, mortar and pestle, and other laboratory equipment. "Not this cupboard, either," he decided.

The fireplace seemed to interest him. The inside he ruled out because the heat from a fire might ruin a notebook. He eyed the stones above the mantel.

"Now that is a very curious thing," he said slowly. "A very curious thing. And to think I never noticed it afore this."

Cherry held her breath. "What didn't you notice?"

"They aren't the same kind of stones at all," he said. "Not at all." He darted across the room, got a straight chair, which he dragged over to the fireplace. Climbing on it, he began feeling the stones just below the legend: "All nature hath a tongue. E'en the stones do speak if ye have ears to hear."

Cherry heard Tammie murmuring to himself as he touched the stones, "This is a rock with gold in it; this one has lapis in it—I can see streaks of platinum. This is quartz." He skipped several he did not appear to know. Then continued, "This one . . . this black one." He stopped, poked the stone harder. "Why, why here's a loose one!" he cried, grasping it with his hands. It was about the size of a large grapefruit. "Look! Look!" He gave it a yank and it fell with a thud on the hearth.

Cherry sprang closer to the boy. And the two of them found themselves staring into a hollowed-out place back of where the stone had been.

"I think there's something in there," Tammie said. His voice rose excitedly, as he started to reach in.

"Don't put your hand in there," Cherry warned, grabbing his arm. Snatching her flashlight from the table where she had left it, she shone it into the hollow. There was something way at the back!

Before she could stop him this time, Tammie jerked his arm free and, reaching in, pulled out a small leather pouch. Jumping down, he handed it to her and they rushed over to the table to look at it by the light of the candelabra. The pouch had a simple drawstring closing, but Cherry's fingers trembled so with excitement that she could not open it. As she fumbled with it, she could feel what seemed to be pebbles inside and something thin and crackling.

"Open it, Miss Ames," Tammie kept saying, hopping about. "Please open it. Let's see what's inside."

"I'm trying," Cherry told him. "But I'm so excited. . . . There!" She pulled the mouth of the pouch open, almost ripping the ancient leather in her haste. The contents—black pellets, some large, some small—spilled out on the table.

Tammie seized one and made white shiny streaks on it by scratching it against his metal belt buckle. "Siller! It's siller!" he cried, dancing up and down. "We found us a whole pocketful of siller!" Pointing toward the black stone which had fallen on the floor, he began to laugh, delighted with himself and his discovery. "That's a siller rock," he declared. "Old Sir Ian hid the pouchful of siller behind the rock with siller in it." He thought it was a wonderful joke. Cherry laughed with him.

She and Tammie picked up a handful of the blackened silver pieces and let them dribble through their fingers. "We've found the treasure, just as people always did in fairy tales, eh, Tammie?"

He nodded, bright-eyed.

Cherry felt the pouch. "There is still something in here," she said, putting her hand inside and drawing out a sheet of paper, folded several times. It had been torn from a notebook, for one edge was ragged. With Tammie watching her intently, Cherry carefully opened the yellowed and fragile sheet, which was covered with writing in a clear, copperplate script, the ink brown with age. She read aloud:

" 'June 8. This is silver from the Old Mine, which has not been worked for years and years. Found rocks of native silver when I went past the crawlway in Rogues' Cave.

" 'June 9. Found more rocks. Pure black sulphurets. When I exposed them to fire, I got globules of native silver. Must be a vein of silver somewhere.

" 'June 10. Followed the tunnel to the shaft of the Old Mine and came out on top of the big hill. Can't find the vein, but brought back more rocks. Each day I melt the silver and hide it behind the stone of silver which I got from the Old Mine. No one would think to look behind this stone above the fireplace. Magic words cannot open Ian Barclay's treasure cranny, as Ali Baba did in the story in Arabian Nights.

" 'June 11. Rained today. The Cameron and Morgan boys came over. They looked at the different rocks I had put under the legend over the fireplace. They did not know one rock from another. They only know about iron.

" 'June 12. Explored all afternoon. Still could not find vein of silver. Mother and Da will be away tomorrow, I shall explore all day. I will find the silver lode. It has to be there.' "

That was the end of the entries.

"A silver mine!" exclaimed Cherry.

"That's what they were looking for, the Bad Ones!" cried Tammie. "Siller!"

"Of course, that's it!" agreed Cherry. "That's what they must be smuggling out."

"The men on the *Heron* have been digging and carrying siller out," said Tammie.

"But, Tammie," Cherry said, "it must take lots and lots of rocks to make a very little silver."

The boy gave her a scornful look. "Ye see that rock," he asked, pointing to the black rock on the hearth. "That's real native siller. It's full of nails, like wire, and they're pure siller. My da says I know the different rocks and minerals almost as well as he does."

"I'll take your word for it," Cherry told him. "But how do these men dig it out? Don't they have to have drills or something?"

"Na, na. Not native siller," replied Tammie. "Ye can dig it out with a bar with a point at one end and a chisel at the other, easy as that." He snapped his fingers. "And it doesn't take a lot to make a good bit of siller, either. My da says some of the miners in Mexico used to hollow out the handles of their hammers and fill them with pulverized rocks. Why, they even, some of them, Da said, used to carry enough away in their cigarette papers to sell for several pennies."

It was obvious Tammie knew what he was talking about. He was apparently as much of a boy scientist as Old Sir Ian had been in his day.

Cherry could scarcely believe that she and the boy Tammie had finally uncovered the secret of the abandoned mine. Of course, the discovery of a rich vein of silver could mean a fortune to the Barclays and probably solve all Sir Ian's financial problems. If Little Joe Tweed's men had been working the vein and carrying off the silver, they must be stopped.

Cherry gathered up the little silver balls and the pages of the notebook and put them back into the leather pouch. "Oh, if only Lloyd and Meg were here!" she thought. She put the pouch into her pocket for safekeeping.

While Cherry had been lost in thought, gathering up the silver pellets, Tammie had been walking up and down in front of the bookshelves.

"Are you looking for something, Tammie?" she asked.

He glanced at her, smiling, "Ay. We dinna find Sir Ian's notebook yet."

"Do you think it's there among the other books?" asked Cherry. She skimmed the titles in their neat rows in the ornate bookcase. Geology and other books on science were all together. Then there were history, biography, fairy tales and ballads, stories of pirates, and factual accounts of explorers and expeditions.

"When I dinna want anyone to find something," Tammie said, peering up under the shelves, "I fix it to the underside of something. There was once a boy who used to swipe my marbles, so I taped the bag under my desk and he caudna find them."

The shelves were of heavy wood, decorated with carving. A strip of carving perhaps three inches wide ran along the front edge of each shelf. Cherry joined Tammie in peering under the shelves behind the strip of carving, which was quite wide enough to hide a book.

Tammie knelt down to look at the second shelf from the floor. "Here's something!" he cried.

Cherry quickly got her flash, and kneeling down beside the boy, played the light on the shelf. She saw that a wooden box with one side cut away had been nailed to the underside of the shelf. Tammie reached in through the cutaway side and pulled out an old book.

Cherry and Tammie grinned happily at each other. He handed the book to her and they slowly stood up. Cherry took the book to the table and together they examined it under the candlelight.

On the spine were the words "The Bo Ha'." The binding was handmade of white canvas now yellow with age, and on the cover in hand lettering was the full title "Sir Greysteel of Bo Ha'."

With rising excitement, Cherry turned back the cover. The first page was filled with handwriting wonderfully clear, even though the paper was yellow and the black ink turned brown. She read aloud to Tammie:

" 'My journal from my 11th Birthday, 21 June 1881. I am going to keep a daily journal beginning today. I shall set down in it what I do and think and things that happen. I shall tell about exploring and all I find and experiment with, such as, plants, bugs, chemicals, but especially rocks and minerals. I mean to be a scientist some day.

" 'I think it amusing to make a jest of my journal, which is all about real things and happenings, and give it a fairy-tale name, Sir Greysteel of Bo Ha'.' "

Cherry read no further.

"Is this the notebook Old Sir Ian used to write in every day when he was a boy?" asked Tammie.

"Yes, Tammie," Cherry told him excitedly. "This is Old Sir Ian's secret journal. And you are the one, Tammie, who found it!"

With trembling fingers, Cherry turned the pages. "See, Tammie," she said, "the pages are filled with writing. And here at the end is where a page has been torn out. That is the page we found in the leather pouch with the silver—it just matches the book. It was the last page he ever wrote in his journal."

Cherry could guess why the torn-out page was the last of the journal. Obviously, the boy had written no more after the time he had been lost for days in Rogues' Cave. He had been quite ill after that experience. And, as soon as he was well enough to travel, he had been sent to school in Scotland. It was twenty years before he returned to Balfour, a man grown and married, so the story went as Higgins had told Cherry. The secret journal and the secret cranny of silver, if Old Sir Ian ever thought of them again, were a part of the long-ago past, better left undisturbed among the magical adventures of boyhood.

Cherry became aware that Tammie's attention had wandered. His head was cocked, listening. The two of them had been so intent on the journal that they had not noticed how quiet everything had become. It would have been quite still outside were it not for the pounding of the surf upon the rocks below the cliffs.

Tammie padded over to the window, opened the casement, and looked out. "I think the storm's almost over," he announced.

Cherry followed and stood beside him to gaze at the sky which was full of clouds racing away to the northeast. Now and then a star shone. But the wind still tossed the branches of the trees and the rain spattered their faces.

"Listen, Miss Ames!" Tammie cried suddenly. "I heard someone cry out down below."

Cherry listened. Faintly, as from a great distance, it seemed she could hear a cry. She was not sure, for the waves roared too loudly.

"There it was again!" exclaimed Tammie. "I heard somebody cry out. It must be Grandda."

Tammie darted away. Cherry leaned out, trying to catch the sound of a voice. When she turned to see what Tammie was doing, she found that he had drawn on his boots and was putting on his slicker.

"I'm going to find Grandda," Tammie said. Snatching up his sou'wester and his bundle, he dodged past her out the door, and went flying down the stairs.

"Tammie! Tammie!" Cherry shouted.

She might as well have called to the wind. Tammie's footsteps could be heard going down, down, down the flights of stairs. The door on the ground floor slammed shut after him, the bang echoing up the stair well.

Cherry had quickly blown out the candles, and, taking her flashlight, raced after him as fast as she could, down the staircase and outside into the storm.

As she ran, she kept calling, "Tammie! Wait! Tammie, wait! You'll get hurt!" But there was no answer.

She went stumbling along the path at the top of the cliffs, shining her flash this way and that, hoping to pick out his figure in the gloom. She called, "Tammie!" No answer. There was no one on the cliffs. She stopped to listen. The only sounds were those of wind and rain and the boom of the surf.

When Cherry burst into the kitchen, drenched, curls in wild disorder, Tess, the cook, was so much startled that she cried out in alarm.

"Oh, Miss Cherry! What's happened?" Tess asked. "You're pale as a ghost!"

"It's Tammie!" Cherry cried out. "Little Tammie Cameron. He's gone. I can't find him. I've looked everywhere."

Higgins, who was just returning from a tour of the downstairs windows to see if water had seeped in, heard their voices raised in alarm and came running. He was aghast to find Cherry, who was supposed to be quite dry inside the house, appear of a sudden all wet and dripping pools of water upon the floor like the King of the Golden River.

The fire in the kitchen fireplace burned up brightly, but Tess and Higgins stood holding candles aloft as if frozen at attention while Cherry breathlessly told them of going to the tower, of Tammie's arrival, of hearing someone call from below the cliffs, of Tammie rushing out in the belief that it was his grandfather, and of her own fruitless search for the boy.

Neither Tess nor Higgins asked questions. To find the boy was the important thing.

In spite of his years, Higgins moved with the agility of youth. Setting down his candle, he plucked his sou'wester and oilskins from a peg on the kitchen wall, and put them on. Then he drew on his boots.

"Smith and Ramsay," Higgins said, referring to the chauffeur and the gardener, "are at the stone cottage. I'll get them and we'll scour the place."

Cherry was all for going with him, but Tess's strong arms restrained her. "Na, na, Miss Cherry," Tess said. "Ye waud only hamper the men."

Higgins went out into the storm. Cherry and Tess watched him until the darkness swallowed up the glow of his flashlight as he ran toward the stone cottage beyond the west gardens where Smith lived with Hugh Ramsay and his wife.

"Get off those wet clothes and take a hot bath," Tess ordered Cherry then, "before ye catch your death." The sturdy, motherly Scotswoman bundled her off upstairs.

Cherry tiptoed to Sir Ian's door and peeked in. It was with profound relief that she saw that Sir Ian was asleep. There was a fire in the fireplace and the room was snug and warm.

That Sir Ian should have slept during all that time, and in the storm with all its noise, struck Cherry as remarkable. She looked at her watch. It was twenty minutes past midnight. With all that had happened, it seemed years since she had gone up to the tower room. Actually it was less than two hours ago.

In her own room, Cherry took the leather pouch

with its pieces of silver and the page torn from the secret journal, from the pocket of her uniform where it had remained safe throughout her frantic chase after Tammie. She put the pouch with its contents in the top drawer of her bureau. Then she took a hot shower and changed into dry, clean clothes.

Tess came up with a bowl of hot soup and crackers on a tray.

"Sit ye doon and drink this," she ordered, placing the tray on a table and drawing a chair alongside.

Cherry did as she was bid, grateful to Tess for her thoughtfulness. Tess selected a straight chair from which she could observe Cherry, and perched on it.

At about Cherry's fourth spoonful of soup, Tess said abruptly, "Now, Miss Cherry, ye'll tell me how it happened that ye and Tammie Cameron were up in the tower this night."

Cherry swallowed the soup. Tess and Higgins had been in the Barclay family so long, she reflected, that they must know just about everything there was to know. So she told Tess the whole story of going up to look for Old Sir Ian's secret journal and of how Tammie had arrived with food for his grandfather who had stowed away on the *Heron.*

"Jock Cameron and his grandson Tammie will be found cold and dead on the Craigmoddie Rocks, most likely." Tess wagged her head in the most doleful manner.

"Oh, don't say that, Tess!" Cherry exclaimed, horrified at the very thought of such a tragedy.

"I waudna say it, if I dinna think it," Tess said with a sigh. "And now that ye tell me Jock stowed away aboard the *Heron*, it's unlikely that he will be heard of again. They've both been kidnaped and spirited away on the fishing boat, ne'er more to be seen."

On this illogical and dismal note, Tess gathered up the dishes and the tray. Admonishing Cherry to try to get some rest, "while ye can, for ye canna tell what tomorrow will bring," the cook took her departure.

Cherry was so depressed over the imaginary fate of Tammie and his grandfather that she immediately burst into tears as soon as Tess left. Then she realized how silly it was. With Higgins, Smith, and Ramsay searching for Tammie, surely he would be found. Besides, Old Jock and Tammie knew the island as well as they did the palm of their hands. As for being kidnaped—that was just Tess speaking out of her dour nature.

It was ridiculous to believe that the *Heron's* crew had made off with Old Jock and little Tammie. So far as Cherry knew, the *Heron* had not even come into port. But where had the fishing boat gone, with Old Jock, the stowaway, and Little Joe Tweed aboard, after leaving St. John's?

"I do know one thing, though," she told herself, drying her eyes and blowing her nose vigorously, "Old Sir Ian found native silver in that Old Mine."

She felt she could no longer sit still and continue to puzzle over things. She would go up to the tower on the chance that Tammie had gone back there and get Old Sir Ian's journal which she had left on the table.

Taking her flashlight, she once more made her way up to the top of the tower. She lighted the candelabra on the table again and looked about. There was no one there, of course. The odor of melted wax and burned wicks hung heavy in the air from her previous visit.

A picture of the little figure in his oilskins rose before her eyes and she was filled with despair when she recalled how he had vanished into the stormy night. Going to a window, she looked out to see if she could catch a glimpse of the lights of the three men, searching for Tammie on the cliffs. She could see nothing. It was dark, the sky still obscured by racing clouds. The wind wailed about the walls of the tower, though the storm seemed spent and the earlier uproar had subsided.

She left the window, picked up the journal, and blowing out the candles made her way back downstairs.

Upon looking into Sir Ian's room, she found him asleep, appearing very comfortable and relaxed.

"I'm wide awake," Cherry thought, "so I might as well sit in here as in my own room." She settled herself in the chair by the fire.

She opened the journal where she had left off and began to read of the daily thoughts and happenings of a boy who lived in that same house so long ago.

After a while the writing blurred on the page. Cherry closed her smarting eyes for a few minutes to rest them. Her head nodded several times and she leaned it against the back of the chair. She fell sound asleep.

CHAPTER XIII

The Wreck

CHERRY WOKE, STARTLED, TO FIND THAT THE CANDLE had long since burned out and only a blob of wax remained in the holder. While she slept, daylight had crept into the room. The journal lay open in her lap to the page where she had left off reading.

She turned her head to look at her patient and saw Sir Ian gazing at her with a fatherly smile.

"Did my heart good to see ye sleeping like a bairn," he commented.

Cherry grinned back at him sheepishly and rubbed her eyes. "I was reading and all of a sudden . . ." Her voice trailed off. Into her mind leaped her worry over Tammie. She must find out at once whether he had been found. She was on the point of springing from her chair when Sir Ian's calm tones brought her back to herself.

"You fell asleep," Sir Ian was saying. "I slept like a top myself. And I feel grand. I'm going to get up."

"Now, you mustn't," Cherry admonished. "It's

too early. Goodness! What time *is* it?" She looked at her watch. It was not quite seven o'clock.

There were sounds of footsteps in the hall and, in a moment, Dr. Mackenzie thrust his tousled head inside the doorway. His face was gray with fatigue, his clothes rumpled. But he appeared in good spirits.

"Barometer's rising and the storm's practically over," he announced. Then he said to Cherry, "Tess told me I'd find you here," and to Sir Ian, "What are you doing awake at this hour?"

"Why shouldn't I be after a long night's rest?" retorted the mine owner.

"Did you ever see such a contrary old Scotsman?" Dr. Mac asked Cherry, with a wink of an eye bloodshot from lack of sleep. "The storm and turmoil kept everyone else on the island up."

"If ye are speaking for yourself, Mackenzie," said Sir Ian, "I can well believe it. From the looks of ye, I'd vow ye'd not touched head to pillow in a week."

"It seems that long," the other agreed ruefully. "Well, I'm glad to see you so chipper, Sir Ian." He walked over to the bed to have a good look at his patient. "Color's good," he commented. Then he took Sir Ian's pulse and nodded with satisfaction. "How do you feel?" he asked.

"Hungry," replied Sir Ian.

"Good. But how do you feel generally speaking?" insisted the doctor.

"If ye canna tell I feel grand this morn," the other replied in his richest Scottish burr, with a wicked little grin, "I dinna think ye are muckle of a medical mon."

With that he tossed back the covers and swung his long, pajama-clad legs off the bed, and began putting on his robe.

"Sir Ian has been giving every indication of getting well," Cherry replied, "including behaving in a very independent manner. He was busy for hours in the library yesterday."

"Are ye through discussing me?" demanded Sir Ian, glaring at them, but with a merry twinkle in his eye. "I'd count it a favor for the both of ye to get out and let a man dress."

"Seeing that by your own expert diagnosis, you are feeling strong and well, sir," said Dr. Mac with exaggerated stiffness, "I am no longer in doubt about asking a favor of you and of Cherry." His tone changed and he became completely serious. "Cherry, you did get some rest, didn't you?"

"Yes, I did, Doctor," Cherry replied.

"Ask your favor and be done," Sir Ian said bluntly.

"We need a nurse badly," Dr. Mac said. "Nurse Cowan, Meg, and the others are pretty worn out, although we all managed to get a little rest off and on."

"What's happened?" asked Sir Ian, instantly alert.

The doctor told briefly of a night spent caring for casualties of the storm. A small pleasure craft had capsized and the six aboard had been rescued and brought to the hospital for treatment. There were a number of serious accidents. People had been injured by flying objects and fallen wires. A good many had had to be treated for exposure and shock. As a result, the hospital had been jammed.

Meg had worked along with Bess Cowan, several

practical nurses, and volunteers. Between them all, they had been able to cope with the situation.

"Why didn't you call me, Dr. Mackenzie?" asked Cherry. "I would have been glad to help."

"I would have, Nurse Ames, but this telephone along with a lot of others was out of order," he explained. "This morning I had to have some professional nursing help. That's why I drove up from the hospital to see how things were here. If it's possible I'd like you to come along with me right away."

"Don't worry about me," Sir Ian said. "I'll be all right. Tess and Norah surely can do anything that's needed. Nurse lass, do ye want to go help in the emergency?"

Cherry nodded emphatically. "Of course I do," she declared. "What is it, Dr. Mac?"

Briefly he explained, "I received a call from the lighthouse just before I came here. Its telephone has been in operation throughout the storm. A fishing boat, the keeper reported, had piled up on the rocks off Carse Point. The Coast Guard have been trying since the boat was sighted earlier this morning, to bring the crew ashore. But the waves have been so high, they've not made much headway up to now. We're going to have to give some medical treatment right there on the beach as the men are brought ashore."

"Fishing boat?" asked Cherry, suddenly suspicious that it might be the *Heron*. "Do you know the name of the boat?"

The doctor shook his head. "No. I didn't ask."

"I'll get ready," Cherry said quickly. Picking up

the secret journal from the table, she crossed the hall to her own room, where she put the book away in the drawer with the leather pouch.

She heard Dr. Mac extracting a promise from Sir Ian that he would not overdo and would eat the bland foods prescribed at regular intervals.

"Remember you are still on a carefully planned regimen until you graduate to the usual three meals a day," warned the doctor.

"I'll bear it in mind," Sir Ian promised. "Now, get along about your business and leave me to bathe and dress."

Cherry got her raincoat, for it was damp and misty out, put on her rubbers and rain hat, and joined Dr. Mac in the hall. She called back to Sir Ian that she would be home as soon as she could.

"You'd better have some breakfast," the doctor cautioned her as they went downstairs. "And I could do with a cup of hot coffee myself."

Anxious to find out if Tess had heard anything more of Tammie, Cherry sprinted toward the kitchen.

"Take it easy. Take it easy," the doctor said, trying to keep up with her.

Tess looked up from stirring the oatmeal mush as they entered. Anticipating Cherry's question, she shook her head in a woebegone way and said, "They've na found the boy. His grandma, Janet Cameron, poor woman is fair daft with worry. She's out there somewhere with the men, searching. I caudna stop her. She waud go."

"What's all this about Janet Cameron's grandson?" asked Dr. Mackenzie.

Tess made them sit down at the table in the kitchen to eat their breakfast before she would answer his question. Then over orange juice, a bowl of mush and milk, and hot coffee, Cherry, at Tess's insistence, began the story of Tammie and the cook finished it. She wound up with the prediction that not only poor Tammie and his grandda, Old Jock, would never be seen again, but that now poor Janet, his grandma, would either catch her death of cold or fall to her death over the cliffs.

Cherry felt her eyes begin to smart with unshed tears, but Dr. Mackenzie took an optimistic view.

"I know that boy, Tammie," he said, "and he's smart as a whip. He can take care of himself on this island as well as any man. He's probably perfectly safe with his grandfather somewhere. As for the two being kidnaped by the crew of the *Heron*—that sounds ridiculous."

Tess sniffed. "I'll not argue with ye, Dr. Douglas Mackenzie," she said smugly.

"They had good reason to kidnap Jock Cameron and Tammie, so it isn't ridiculous at all, Dr. Mac," Cherry declared, siding with Tess. "Mr. Cameron discovered that the crew has been smuggling something out through Rogues' Cave. I have good reason to believe it is silver."

"Silver!" cried Dr. Mackenzie, starting to laugh and choking over his last swallow of coffee. "Don't tell me you don't know the story of the silver in Rogues' Cave!"

"You know about the *silver?*" asked Cherry incredulously.

"Of course," replied the doctor, still sputtering with suppressed laughter. "I'm surprised that someone hasn't told you that old story before this."

Cherry's face must have shown clearly her utter astonishment, for he hastened to correct himself, "No, I don't suppose you would hear of it."

Tess walked over with the pot of coffee to fill up the doctor's cup. She said stiffly, "Ye were about to speak, Dr. Mac, of the men—ah, what blackguards they were!—who salted the Old Mine with silver. Weel, 'tis a common enough story in the village. But 'tis na heard in Barclay House. Neither is it one that's told where a Barclay might hear it."

"Then, Tess, I shall tell it to Miss Ames on the way to Carse Point," retorted the doctor. "It does the Barclays good, as well as most everyone else, to learn to laugh at themselves once in a while."

During the exchange between Tess and Dr. Mac, Cherry quietly ate her oatmeal and drank her coffee. Already worried about Tammie and Old Jock, she knew that Dr. Mac's story would send her spirits even lower. She had only a vague idea of what salting a mine meant. But it was associated in her mind with nothing particularly pleasant.

"I'm ready to go, if you are, Dr. Mac," she said, getting up. She praised Tess's oatmeal as being "just right."

"Thank you, Tess, for making me eat one of your delicious breakfasts," said the doctor. "Let's go, Cherry."

Tess promised to leave word at the hospital or the

lighthouse if she learned anything new about Tammie. The cook had little hope, however, that telephone service at Barclay House would be restored soon.

"The lines are doon, a great tangle of wires, Ramsay, the gardener, told me when I saw him early this morning," she reported. "So 'tis na likely ye'll be hearing from me a-tall."

Cherry and the doctor went outside to his Ford.

"It's good of you to come," Dr. Mac said, once they were on the road to Carse Point Lighthouse. "You know it's no part of your duty to do this."

"So long as my patient is all right and you, his doctor, say it's all right," Cherry told him, smiling, "I would not be much of a nurse if I did not do what I could in an emergency like this."

Dr. Mac gave her a grateful smile in return. "You're a real nurse, Cherry Ames," he complimented her. "And a wonderful person."

As they bumped along the road beside the cliffs, Cherry asked if he had forgotten that he was to tell her about the silver in Rogues' Cave.

"Certainly not," he answered, and began, "You've heard of George Barclay, Sir Ian's brother, of course. He's the one who lives off the fat of the land in England."

Cherry told him she had.

"Well, he's a later edition of a George Barclay who was born a number of years after the Old Mine was closed. The early George, like this later one, was a spendthrift and always in debt. Somehow or other he made the acquaintance of a slick grafter, a silver prospector, who had been fooling around in the silver mines in Mexico. This grafter persuaded Meg and Lloyd's Great-great-uncle George Barclay to let him explore Rogues' Cave for gold and silver, promising to make George rich quick. The grafter spent a lot of time in the cave, then came out one day, whooping and hollering that he'd found silver. Well, sir, when Great-great-uncle George went in there with the grafter, sure enough, there were all these rocks of native silver. Uncle George rewarded the man handsomely. The grafter left the island in a hurry, before Uncle George could discover that the rocks of native silver had been planted there. In fact, the fellow had brought the few rocks from Mexico for the purpose. In short, Great-great-uncle George Barclay had been played for a sucker, to put it bluntly. The grafter had salted the mine, as it is called, which was a common thing in those days. And many a seasoned miner or even an old prospector was taken in by a cleverly salted mine."

Cherry sighed deeply. "I suppose Sir Ian's father simply found some of these rocks, too, when he was a boy," she said to herself. The excitement which had been building up inside her ever since she and Tammie had found the leather pouch in the tower room, collapsed within her like a spent balloon. She really had nothing at all to tell Meg and Lloyd now.

And there probably would be no need to tell them about the disappearance of Tammie and Old Jock, for the news would have filtered through to them from some of the islanders by this time.

Cherry said, "Oh, dear," with a sigh that went to the soles of her nurse's shoes.

"Did you say something?" asked Dr. Mackenzie.

"No, I was just thinking what a joke it is about the silver," she answered. "It's such an old joke, it has whiskers on it." She laughed without humor.

"You don't make it sound cheerful," observed the doctor. "Now, come on, Nurse Ames. Just think of Great-great-uncle George as a gay dog with much money and little wit, who paid for a needed lesson from another gay dog with plenty of wit and no money. How's that for an early-day Mackenzie gem of an aphorism?"

Cherry laughed this time with good humor.

The island looked different after the storm. In the pale yellow of a sun obscured by clouds, everything appeared tossed and tumbled about as in a giant washing machine. The trees and bushes were bent and twisted. Buildings displayed broken windows like missing teeth, a fallen chimney, or wind-ripped cornices. From the sea came the pounding of the waves upon the rocks and sandy beaches.

They were some distance from Carse Point when they could see the crowd which had gathered on the shore near the lighthouse. Presently they could make out the Canadian Coast Guard cutter standing by offshore.

Drawing nearer, Cherry and the doctor saw the fishing boat, clothed in spray, stationary on the rocks where she had been left by the high tides of the storm. Around the vessel the waters boiled and foamed.

The Coast Guard had finally got a line aboard the boat, from the shore to the bridge of the ship, and had rigged the breeches buoy. They had started to bring the crew ashore as Cherry and Dr. Mac drove up.

There were an ambulance, stretchers and folding cots, blankets—all in readiness. There were a chest with first-aid and other medical supplies and plenty of warm water, soap, and sterile cloths.

At one side, a group of women had set up a field kitchen, and were serving hot coffee, tea, and sandwiches to the lifesavers. Later, hot drinks and food would be given to the rescued.

With the exception of the men on the Coast Guard cutter, those manning the breeches buoy, and the lighthouse keeper, the lifesavers were volunteers, citizens of Balfour.

Scarcely anyone noticed Cherry and the doctor as they walked over to where the men were hauling in the first of the crew aboard the wrecked boat. Every head was turned to watch the man in the breeches buoy skimming over the white-capped waves in a device that resembled a baby's walker attached to an overhead cable.

As soon as the fisherman was near enough for Cherry to get a good look at him, she exclaimed, "Oh, doctor, his left leg's broken!"

Her cry caused the crowd that had been watching silently to turn to look at her and the doctor. People called greetings to the two of them.

"Here's Dr. Mac now," one of the bystanders called out. "He's got Nurse Ames with him."

By this time everyone on the island knew Cherry Ames, Sir Ian's nurse, either by sight or from hearing about her.

The crowd made way for the doctor and Cherry to go over to where the men were gently lifting the fisherman out of the buoy. Dr. Mackenzie signaled to two men with a stretcher, and the injured man was eased onto it.

The man's face was distorted with pain. His trouser leg had been cut away and a crude splint had been applied to the leg.

As the doctor removed splint and bandage carefully, the man explained, "The captain fixed me up after I broke it."

The foot was turned outward and the ankle and leg were badly swollen. The man winced as the doctor felt it very gently.

"What's your name?" the doctor asked.

"Jim Freeman," replied the other. "I was sent ashore first because I was hurt worse than the rest."

"Well, I'm going to give you something to ease your pain," Dr. Mac told him, taking out his hypodermic needle. As he gave the injection, he went on talking, "But that's a bad break, Mr. Freeman, and it will have to be X-rayed. I'm going to send you to the hospital in the ambulance."

Cherry saw where the end of the broken bone had penetrated through the skin and knew it was a compound fracture. The doctor could not determine the extent of the injury without X rays. The captain's attempt to splint and bandage the leg, although no doubt well-intentioned, had not been beneficial in this case. For a simple fracture where the bone was broken but not separated, a splint to hold the bone in place would have been effective.

Cherry cleansed the wound and covered it with a loose bandage. Jim Freeman was wrapped warmly and sent off to the hospital, where Nurse Cowan would take X rays and look after him until the doctor came.

The waters were gradually subsiding, although they remained too rough for the Coast Guard cutter to draw near enough to the wreck to take off the crew. However, the men at the breeches buoy worked more quickly and one after the other of the bruised and battered men were brought ashore.

Folding cots had been set up on the beach and the men were placed on them. Those suffering from shock and exposure or slight injuries were warmly covered and given warm drinks by the women volunteers. The beach around the lighthouse soon took on the appearance of a hospital ward.

Cherry and Dr. Mac worked together, treating the serious cases. A man with a dislocated shoulder took all the doctor's strength, with Cherry helping him, to get the end of the upper arm bone, the humerus, to snap back into its socket. Another had a severe bruise with much swelling and pain which the doctor treated with one of the newly developed medicines for the purpose. The ship's cook had received a third-degree burn on his arms and hands when a kettle of boiling water overturned.

Still another had an ugly cut along the side of his

neck, which he had wrapped in a none-too-clean piece of cloth. He was pale from loss of blood.

To the doctor's question if he had been in the armed forces and been immunized by an injection of tetanus toxoid against lockjaw, the man replied yes.

Cherry removed the bandage very carefully and the doctor took a look at the wound. As he was examining it the lifesavers at the breeches buoy called out that the man they had been hauling ashore had collapsed.

"Doctor, please come quick," they cried.

"Think you can take care of this man, with the cut?" Dr. Mackenzie asked Cherry. "Sew up the cut; give him an injection of toxoid. Since he has already been immunized against tetanus, all he needs is a booster shot."

Cherry nodded. "Yes, Doctor, I know how."

He handed her a bottle, the needle for the injection, and hurried off to the shore where the man lay immobile on the sand.

Cherry bent over the man with the cut, who had been placed on a cot, to get a closer look at the wound.

"Fell on a piece of sharp metal of some kind on the boat during the storm," he answered in response to her question of how he had received the bad cut. The edge of the metal had barely missed the jugular vein.

Others on nearby cots, who had come through relatively unscathed, took up the story of the previous night. They had been coming up from St. John's. The storm had hit them when they were a mile or so north of the Craigmoddie Rocks at the southeast end of the island.

"I thought we were going to sink any minute," one of them said. "The captain decided we couldn't come round and make it through the pass and into Balfour Harbor. So we headed north, only to be driven onto the rocks at Carse Point at the other end of the island."

Cherry heard them talking, but her first attention was given to her work.

She washed the long, deep cut with soap and water, then with warm water. From the little cylinder-like bottle the doctor had given her, she took sterile surgical thread and needle and neatly sewed the skin together. It was the first time that she had ever done such a serious cut alone, but she was so familiar with the technique that her fingers moved confidently.

She was just finishing when the doctor passed with his patient on a stretcher. He stopped, briefly examined her work, and said, "I couldn't have done better myself. Now, I'm going to have to leave you in charge here for a while. The man who collapsed just now was the last man aboard. Name's Banghart. He's the captain. He's had a heart attack. I've given him an injection to ease the pain, but I must get him to the hospital and into the oxygen tent right away. Think you can look after the others? There are no serious injuries. I'll be back as soon as possible."

"I think I can manage, Dr. Mac," Cherry replied. "I'll do my best."

"That's a pretty high rating in my book," Dr. Mackenzie said with a smile. "No one could ask for more." And he went on to the ambulance with his patient.

Cherry continued with her work, putting on a sterile pad over the injured area, then made a cravat type of bandage which covered the injury and went over and around to hold the pad in place. She then gave him an injection, or booster dose of toxoid as a safety measure, as the doctor had instructed her.

A group of people had grown about the wounded, although everyone was standing back so as not to interfere with Cherry. They watched her with respect and admiration as she moved from one patient to another.

While she went about her work, Cherry heard the group of islanders and the crew talking back and forth. She gathered that the Balfourians knew a good many of the crew, for they called the various fishermen by name. The fishermen gave only brief or evasive answers to the probing questions.

Close by, Cherry heard one of the islanders and one of the crew in an exchange.

"I think ye said ye had thirty-six aboard, counting the captain," said the islander. "But I counted less than that brought ashore. What became of the other poor lads. Did they drown?"

"Probably," replied the other.

"Why probably. Don't ye know?" persisted his questioner.

"The mate, Mr. Tweed, and some others lowered a boat and rowed for shore," came the answer. "I don't think they could make it in the storm, so they probably drowned."

"I noticed the mate was missing," remarked the Balfourian. "Weel, now, he may be alive—he and the others—the same as the rest of ye." The man paused.

With his next words, Cherry's heart began to thump with excitement.

The Balfourian continued, "Ah, 'twaud be a wondrous thing, this wreck, if every man jack aboard the *Heron* was saved!"

"Every man jack aboard the *Heron!*" thought Cherry. The *Heron!* These men she was taking care of were members of the crew of the *Heron*. But some were missing. The mate, Mr. Tweed, and some of the men had lowered a boat and rowed for shore. Had they been drowned or had they reached shore safely? And what had become of Old Jock, who had stowed away?

How she managed to care for the rest of the *Heron's* crew who had slight bruises, scratches and cuts, and sprains, she never knew. But apparently she did her job very well. When Dr. Mac returned that afternoon with a doctor and nurses from St. John's to relieve them, he was amazed to find all but a few of the men perfectly able to return on the *Sandy Fergus* to their homes in St. John's.

Dr. Mac sent Cherry back to Barclay House, saying that he had already sent Meg home, as well as Nurse Cowan, to get some sleep. He himself was going home and to bed before he dropped in his tracks. The doctor and nurses from St. John's, who had arrived on the *Sandy Fergus* in response to his call, were ready to take over for a day or two.

CHAPTER XIV

The Silver of the Mine

THE NEXT MORNING AFTER BREAKFAST, THE FOUR—
Cherry and Lloyd, Meg, and Dr. Mackenzie—stood
in the bright sun on the brow of the cliff, peering
down upon the sparkling waters of the little bay at
Rogues' Cave.

Dressed in sturdy clothes and equipped with ropes
and miners' safety lamps on lanyards round their
necks, and knives in sheaths at their belts, the four
could have been taken for a party of spelunkers—
cave explorers. Prepared for any emergency, Lloyd
had a compass and from his belt hung a geologist's
hammer and pick, and binoculars.

"The tide isn't low enough yet to get into Rogues'
Cave without wading," Lloyd said.

"Then let's start with the entrance to the Old
Mine," suggested Dr. Mac.

In silence they made their way back along the cliffs
and set off up the big hill of the abandoned mine. A

gentle breeze rippled the grass and flirted the brightly colored scarfs of the girls. In the blue, cloudless sky a naval helicopter from the nearby base hovered off-shore, searching for the bodies of the four men missing from the *Heron* and now believed to be drowned.

The presence of the whirlybird was ignored by the group as they climbed the hill. None of them wanted to be reminded that the chances were against their finding Old Jock and Tammie or the missing men, either in the mine or the cave. But Cherry had convinced Lloyd and Meg and Dr. Mac that the search was well worth a try. The fact that Ramsay, the gardener, had found the *Heron's* lifeboat high, dry, and undamaged on the sand dunes on a beach north of the cliffs was taken as a hopeful sign that the men had reached shore.

That morning, after a good night's rest, Cherry, Lloyd, Meg, Dr. Mac (who had come over at Meg's invitation), and Sir Ian had all been present at breakfast in the Barclay dining room.

Sir Ian, who had not been told that Old Jock and Tammie were missing, was in the best of spirits. He had no sooner sat down at the table, then he announced, "I am expecting James Broderick this morning. Just after the telephone line was repaired earlier, Mr. Broderick called and left word with Higgins that he was flying over from St. John's. Mr. Broderick had an appointment to see me the day of the storm, but caudna make it, of course."

"Mr. Broderick is flying over this morning!" Lloyd said, startled. "Could I ask what he's coming for?"

"Ye caud," answered his uncle. "But since it's a

matter strictly between him and me, there's na need
to tell ye, nephew."

There was a glint in Sir Ian's eye as though he
were exhilarated over the coming meeting. Cherry
had never seen the mine owner look stronger or
better than he did that morning. His face was wonderfully alive and he held himself proudly.

"Why, he reminds me of descriptions I've read in
old stories of knights just about to go into battle,"
Cherry thought. "It is as though the prospect of the
battle stimulated them and made them feel full of
confidence."

Sir Ian had eaten his breakfast, without making
any further comment. Then he had gone off to the
library "to do some paper work," he said. He was not
to be disturbed under any circumstances.

After he had left, Cherry had shown Lloyd, Meg,
and Dr. Mac, Old Sir Ian's secret journal and the
leather pouch containing the torn page and the silver.
Then she had told of the night in the tower room
and Tammie's disappearance.

Her suggestion that they search the Old Mine and
Rogues' Cave for Old Jock and Tammie, and at the
same time solve the mystery of the silver, had been
received with enthusiasm by her three listeners.

"I think it's about time we found out what this
whole thing is about," Lloyd had declared at once.

As they pushed their way to the top of the hill now,
each of them was torn between hope one moment and
despair the next of what they might or might not find
in the underground tunnels.

They reached the summit.

Meg and the doctor pushed ahead through the bushes and began to examine the big rock which Cherry had found so interesting on the day Little Joe Tweed had vanished as if by magic.

"Do look, Lloyd," Meg said, "this is the oddest sort of rock. I don't remember ever having seen it here before, not even when we came up here as children."

"Yes, it has a very peculiar texture," Dr. Mac said. "Like pumice."

Lloyd looked at it for the first time. "It *is* pumice," he replied at once.

"That's the rock I was telling all of you about," Cherry said. "Only it has sunk much deeper into the ground since I saw it last—probably washed down by the heavy rain." Turning to Lloyd, she asked, "Did you say it was *pumice?*" Suddenly she remembered a rock she had held in her hand when she and Tammie were in the tower. It had been feather light.

"Why, that's where the entrance to the mine used to be!" exclaimed Meg. "Someone has taken away the old boards that used to cover it and set a rock over it."

Lloyd caught Cherry's eye and they exchanged a significant glance. They both knew the nature of that rock.

With a wink at Cherry, Lloyd announced, "Stand back, everybody, while I give a remarkable demonstration of weight lifting." Suiting his action to his words, he grasped the mass of grayish-colored rock and rolled it aside with little effort.

"Ah, a Hercules!" cried Dr. Mac, laughing.

"As you see," explained Lloyd in a carnival hawker's nasal twang, "it's light as foam, for that is precisely what it is—foam spewed up by a volcano and hardened into rock. It's not native to the island. Somebody brought it here from a faraway volcanic region."

The three applauded Lloyd.

"Well, there's the mouth of the mine shaft," he said, pointing at their feet.

They all looked down into the cavity which had been covered by the rock. The opening was just large enough for a man to enter.

They tied rope about their waists mountain-climber fashion—Lloyd, Cherry, Meg, Dr. Mac—in that order. Then Lloyd eased himself down into the hole, the bottom of which was perhaps six feet below the surface of the ground.

"Okay," he told them in a moment. "There's a ladder leading down, a little way ahead. It's new from the looks of it. Someone built it recently. Definitely, this shaft is being used."

"Switch on your lamps up there," he ordered. "Come on, Cherry. Meg, you and Doc follow."

Cherry slid down into the cavity. Lloyd was already descending the ladder, a few feet in front of her. With her heart thumping in her throat, she slowly, rung by rung, went down to the top level of the mine where Lloyd stood on the dirt floor of the tunnel.

The others joined them and they began exploring the tunnel by the light of their lamps. The tunnel extended to the right and the left, but only for a short distance in each direction. Water dripped from the roof, forming little pools. The earthen floor was muddy and marked with many footprints.

"Men have been going and coming through here

regularly," remarked Lloyd. "Those are men's footprints, as you can readily see, and that's the only thing they can possibly mean. Men enter the shaft by rolling away the rock. When Little Joe Tweed disappeared that day, Cherry, he must have done just that. They came down the ladder, which was made probably to replace an old, rotted one, and they go . . ." He played his flashlight about.

Another ladder in front of them led downward. "Here's where they go," Lloyd said, and began at once to lower himself on it.

They all descended two more ladders before they came to the place where the central shaft of the Old Mine ended and there was no further means of descent. As before, the tunnel extended to the right and to the left. But this time, there was another tunnel cutting in at an angle and sloping gently in a southeasterly direction, so Lloyd told them upon consulting his compass.

"I guess it's a case of counting eeny, meeny, miney, mo, or isn't it, Engineer Barclay?" asked Meg.

"It is not, Miss Barclay," returned Lloyd. "That tunnel running in a southeasterly direction goes toward Rogues' Cave. Notice the footprints. And notice all the shoring is new wood. Notice that the tunnel itself has been recently dug. And let me remind you that Cherry told us that Old Jock wanted to find out what was being smuggled *out through Rogues' Cave.*"

"Lloyd, did the men—whoever they are—dig this tunnel so they could get to the cave?" Cherry asked.

The journey down the tunnel seemed endless

"Exactly," replied Lloyd. "You see, there was never a tunnel that ran to the cave from this mine. There was just the shaft which you see goes straight down from the top of the hill. Then there were tunnels running to the north and south from this shaft, as you saw when we descended."

With Lloyd in the lead, the four walked down the sloping tunnel, the glimmer of their lamps guiding them in the darkness.

The journey down the tunnel seemed endless to Cherry. But Lloyd said they had gone perhaps only a quarter of a mile when they came upon a wall of stone which had been broken through to form a low, jagged doorway.

Lloyd bent his head and was on the point of entering the passage beyond when he drew back quickly.

"There's a light down there a little way and I heard people talking," he said in a whisper filled with suppressed excitement.

Cherry felt her spine tingle. She was so anxious to find out what was beyond the doorway that it was all she could do to restrain her impulse to rush past Lloyd. Meg and Dr. Mackenzie started to whisper questions.

"Sssh," Lloyd warned them. "Don't talk. Follow me without making a sound."

One by one, they went through the doorway. They saw immediately the glow of a light and moved toward it very, very slowly. Then, just beyond a turning, on their left was a sort of large alcove off the tunnel. From the alcove came the sound of men's voices talking in a dull, quiet way.

"Put out your lights," Lloyd said to Cherry and the other two.

Then, in the dark, very cautiously, keeping close to the wall of the tunnel, they crept up to the entrance and peered into the alcove.

The place had been blasted out of the rock and was quite large, though it seemed smaller than it was, for piled up like cordwood about the floor, were sackfuls of what was unmistakably rocks. Among the heaps, four men sat on the floor about a wooden box, playing cards by the light of a miner's lamp.

"That man on the right is Little Joe Tweed," Cherry quickly whispered in Lloyd's ear.

"Yes, I see him," Lloyd whispered back.

"The sea will be calm enough tonight," Little Joe was saying, "to bring our boat into Rogues' Cave. I want to get this silver out of here by tonight. I've worked out a place to have it crushed and the silver extracted and no questions asked. We'll block up the tunnel before we leave, so no one will get wise to the fact we've discovered a silver mine worth a fortune. Then we'll turn up in St. John's with a horrible tale of suffering—of being lost at sea, riding out the storm, and finally reaching shore."

For several moments Cherry had the eerie feeling that someone was looking at them.

Now, letting her glance rove about the room, she gave a joyful little gasp upon encountering two eyes staring at her out of what she had mistaken for a sack of rocks in the shadowy corner. Sitting on the floor with his back against the wall of the alcove, trussed up with rope and gagged, was Old Jock Cameron. She nodded to him to let him know that she had seen him.

Then, clutching Lloyd's arm so he would not move and make a noise, she said in barely audible tones, "Look closely, Lloyd, you'll see Mr. Cameron. You have a knife. If you can get close enough or he can wriggle this way, you can cut him loose."

Lloyd answered by squeezing her hand. Leaning over he said, "Untie the rope around your waist. Tell Meg and Dr. Mac to do the same."

When they were all freed from one another, Lloyd said softly, "Now, here's my plan of action, everybody. Cherry, you and Meg stand against the wall and don't make a sound. Doc, get out your knife. Meg, let me have your knife. As soon as I've cut Old Jock free, I'll whistle just once softly. That's your cue, Doc, to come out fighting. We'll rush Little Joe and his men. None of them seems to be armed. I can't see anything that looks like a gun, can you, Doc?"

Dr. Mac peered at the men a moment. "No." He took his knife out of the sheath. "Well, I'm all set."

"Now, you, Cherry and Meg," said Lloyd. "You get out of here as fast as you can when Dr. Mac and I rush those men in there. We're not going to use our knives, but we are going to try to frighten them enough so they won't give us any trouble. But the Doc and I don't want you girls in this. So get out fast."

"Do we go back the way we came?" asked Meg.

"No, follow the new tunnel," said Lloyd. "It has to lead out through the cave. The smuggling is out through the cave, remember? Just be sure, by playing your lights over the tunnel walls and the wood that it is the newly dug tunnel. It probably leads right into one of the tunnels in the cave that you know, Meg. Everybody all set?" Lloyd asked.

The three said they were.

"Hang on to these," Lloyd told Cherry, giving her his binoculars and geologist's hammer and pick. With that, he dropped to the floor of the tunnel and started crawling toward Old Jock in the alcove. The light was dim and the place was full of shadows.

As the three waited, they heard Little Joe and the others still talking.

"Have you figured out yet what to do with old man Cameron, Little Joe?" asked one.

"The storm caused a lot of accidents—some of them fatal," suggested Little Joe.

This was greeted with general laughter.

A whining voice complained, "Sure, Little Joe, that takes care of the old man, but what about the kid? That night in the storm when we ran after the old man and caught him, we shouldn't have bothered taking the kid. Besides, the kid got away, anyway—a regular eel."

"Never mind the kid." Little Joe brushed the matter aside. "He probably drowned. You told me yourself you saw him disappear just before you reached the cave. Rogues' Cave was filled with water way up over the ledge, you said."

"Yes, but you can't be sure he fell in," the voice whined.

"Forget it," snapped Little Joe.

"Tammie! Oh, my goodness!" Cherry murmured

despairingly. "Poor little Tammie, drowned in Rogues' Cave."

Then it struck her that perhaps he had not drowned at all. Tammie had disappeared just before he had reached the cave, the man had said.

Cherry focused her attention on Lloyd, crawling as slowly as a snail toward Old Jock. He had only a little way to go. Even as Cherry watched, Lloyd was reaching out with his knife to cut the rope that bound Old Jock's ankles. Now, Lloyd had pulled himself alongside Old Jock and was cutting the rope that bound his hands behind him. He handed the knife to Old Jock and took Meg's knife in his hand. Old Jock ripped the gag off his mouth. It had all been done so slowly and quietly that it was like watching a silent film in slow motion.

With a start, Cherry heard a short whistle. It was Lloyd's cue to Dr. Mac. And the doctor sprang from his place against the wall, and darted into the alcove to take his place beside Lloyd and Old Jock.

Little Joe and his three men got up so quickly they knocked over the box on which they were playing cards. Then altogether they started toward Lloyd, Dr. Mac, and Old Jock, who held their knives menacingly in their hands.

Meg grabbed Cherry's arm as the men rushed toward each other and started to grapple. "We must go. Lloyd said we mustn't stay here," she said.

"I know," Cherry said. They switched on their miners' lamps and started off. Meg led the way, flashing her lamp on the walls and boards to see if they were following the newly dug tunnel. They raced along for quite some distance, then Meg stopped suddenly.

"Look!" she said to Cherry. "This is where the new part ends."

The two girls shone the lamps over the sides of the tunnel and they could see clearly where the old shoring was next to the new. Beyond the newly dug part, the tunnel continued, but it had been dug and shored up long ago.

"Listen!" Cherry put her hand on Meg's arm. The two of them stood still for a moment. "I hear the pounding of waves on the shore," Cherry said. "Don't you, Meg?"

"Yes," Meg answered. "We are near Rogues' Cave."

"Meg, we can't be far from the hidey-hole, can we?" asked Cherry.

"I know what you're thinking," Meg said. "Tammie. Tammie may be in the hidey-hole."

They raced down the tunnel, the sound of the sea growing louder and louder in their ears all the time. At last they came to the passage that Cherry remembered from her visit with Meg. They were not far from the hidey-hole.

Cherry began calling, "Tammie! Tammie, where are you!"

Meg was infected by Cherry's desperately hopeful cry that Tammie must be there in the hidey-hole, or in the cave somewhere. Meg took up the call and both girls shouted at the top of their lungs.

The tunnel echoed and re-echoed their call of "Tammie, Tammie, Tammie."

Suddenly ahead of them a little door screeched over the stones. Their lights picked up a small figure in sou'wester, oilskins, and high rubber boots emerging from the hidey-hole.

He cried, "Meg! Oh, Cherry!" and rushing forward flung his arms around them.

Half an hour later, a dismal-appearing group, muddy and dirty from head to foot, went trooping into the hall of Barclay House. They made a great clatter. Cherry and Meg, holding Tammie's hands, marched in first. Then came Little Joe Tweed and the three sullen members of the *Heron's* crew, their hands tied behind their backs. Bringing up the rear were Lloyd, Dr. Mackenzie, and Old Jock, with bags of native silver flung over their shoulders, looking like country peddlers. All the men were dirty, their clothes torn, and bore bruises and scratches.

Higgins on his way downstairs from the second floor was stopped in his tracks at the amazing apparition.

"Where's Uncle Ian?" asked Lloyd at once.

"He's in the library with Mr. Broderick, sir," replied Higgins, mouth agape.

Just then they heard a door open and Sir Ian's voice say, "You may bankrupt *me* if you like, Mr. Broderick, but you'll never get control of the Balfour Mines."

"I wouldn't be too sure of that," said Mr. Broderick firmly.

"I know what I'm talking about and ye don't," said Sir Ian. "For the last couple of days I've been carefully checking over everything I possess. My share in the mines right now will pay just about what I owe the bank. Barclay House and everything in it belong to my daughter Meg. I don't own anything else. Either ye take the payments on the money ye loaned me—and I'll pay several thousand a quarter out of my income, or ye leave it."

"Suppose I choose to leave it," said Broderick.

"Then ye'll be cutting off your nose to spite your face," declared Sir Ian. "Ye won't get your money back and ye won't gain control of the mines, either."

"I don't want to press you too much," Broderick said, sounding slightly disconcerted. "You've been a great man in Canadian mining for too many years and your family before you. I admire your courage, holding onto a family dynasty in these modern times."

"I'm much obliged to ye," said Sir Ian. "I shall act towards ye in good faith, that ye know. Dinna press me and ye'll get every penny coming to ye."

"Well, Sir Ian, I'm a modern businessman," declared Broderick. "I've little patience with outdated methods of mining and paying debts. Unless you can clear up your debts soon, I'll have to take further steps."

"Ye've warned me," said Sir Ian. "Now, good day to ye, sir."

None of the group in the hall had moved. They had listened in fascinated silence.

The next instant, Mr. Broderick came striding toward them. He halted abruptly at the entrance to the hallway. Lloyd, bag over shoulder, went up to him.

"You won't have long to wait, Mr. Broderick,"

Lloyd said. "You'll be paid your money within a very short time, I guarantee it. So it won't be necessary for you to take further steps to collect your money."

"That's it, my lad!" shouted Old Jock encouragingly to Lloyd. "The Barclays have a silver mine. It's a bonanza!"

"Is that true, Mr. Barclay?" Mr. Broderick asked, turning to Lloyd.

"Every word of it," replied Lloyd.

The noise brought Sir Ian storming out of the library. "What in the world is going on here?" he demanded, irate and amazed.

Before anyone else could answer, Mr. Broderick spoke up. "Sir Ian," he said ruefully, "it appears you have a silver mine. A bonanza. And, as your nephew just told me, I'll have the money you owe me very soon. My business definitely is over now. Good day, Sir Ian, Mr. Barclay." Nodding to Meg and Cherry, he started toward the door. Then he turned around suddenly and went up to Little Joe Tweed.

"Mr. Tweed, the other day when you and my pilot, Jerry Ives, came into the coffee shop in St. John's, you said you wanted to make me a proposition. Well, I told you then that any proposition coming from you was bound to be crooked and I refused to let you say anything.

"Afterward, my pilot told me you had run into him on the wharf and began talking about having a lot of native silver to sell. He couldn't get rid of you until he had brought you to see me. Now I know where you must have got the silver. You smuggled it out of the Barclays' mine."

With that, Mr. Broderick started once again toward the door, which Higgins hurried to open, and strode outside. Jerry Ives was waiting in one of the company "Bugs" to take his boss to the Balfour airfield and fly him back to St. John's.

For several minutes after Mr. Broderick's departure, the Barclay hall was in complete turmoil, with Little Joe shouting that Sir Ian had always had it in for him, even when he, Little Joe, was working in the mines. And he was going to fight the Barclays in court. Little Joe's men started to shout, too, and there was a great deal of shouting all round before Smith, the chauffeur, and Ramsay, the gardener, got the men in a car and took them off to the chief of police of the island.

When they had gone, Sir Ian exclaimed, "Now, ye people, tell me what this is all about! A silver mine. Smugglers. Those sacks, ye've brought. Jock here with Tammie. The lot of ye all bedraggled. I've never seen the likes of such a hullabaloo."

"I'll tell you, Uncle," said Lloyd. He turned upon Cherry an admiring look that ignored tangled curls, the streaks of dirt, bedraggled clothes. And he said, "Since Miss Cherry Ames is the real heroine of this occasion, I think she should begin the story. It's called 'The Silver of the Mine.'"

The story that Cherry began was taken up by Old Jock after they had all washed and cleaned up, and were sitting comfortably in the library, waiting for Higgins to announce luncheon.

Old Jock told of becoming suspicious at first of something going on in the Old Mine and in Rogues'

Cave when the series of accidents occurred in No. 2 mine.

"Every time we dug in the direction of the Old Mine," Old Jock said, "something happened. And the same two men always were involved. At least, the other men reported carelessness or negligence by one or the other of these two miners. They were from St. John's and I noticed they were very friendly with Little Joe Tweed. I began to wonder if those two miners had a reason for keeping us from extending Number 2 mine any nearer the Old Mine."

Old Jock explained that a vein of ore, which had been opened, might very well extend into the Old Mine. His vague suspicions led him to do a bit of investigating. Soon he discovered that the *Heron* was frequently offshore. Then he saw a heavily laden rowboat leaving Rogues' Cave. Next he discovered that the Old Mine shaft had been repaired. He had gone down one day only to find two men on guard. He had never been able to get near the alcove where he had been found trussed up. In fact, he had no idea that a vein of silver had actually been found.

Of course he had suspected that some valuable mineral might have been discovered. On the other hand, it was equally possible that the Old Mine and Rogues' Cave were simply being used as a warehouse for smuggling anything of value.

"Why didn't ye let me know about this?" asked Sir Ian.

"Ah, that I caudna, Ian," Old Jock said. "I knew what terrible tension ye have been under for so long. And ye were a sick man. I had to try to clear everything up without involving ye in a lot of worry and anxiety."

Finally he had decided to stow away on the *Heron*. When and if a boat was sent into Rogues' Cave to pick up cargo, Old Jock would manage to get aboard it, for the boat was large with a covered stern beneath which he could hide. He had taken particular note of this when he had watched it while pretending to be fishing all those times.

He had asked Tammie to wait for him in the tower because it was nearest to Rogues' Cave and perfectly safe. If Old Jock found Little Joe and his crew actually engaged in illegal activities, he would simply have Tammie telephone a message to his grandmother. Old Jock and his wife Janet had it all planned what she would tell the chief of police.

"I thought Tammie could phone his grandma without arousing Ramsay's curiosity," Old Jock explained. "But if I went in at night to use his phone, he'd wonder right away what it was all about. But Tammie phoning his grandma of a night—well, Ramsay would think right away that the boy was in trouble with his grandmother because he'd stayed out too late."

"Well," continued Old Jock, "the storm came and worked havoc with my plans."

He had got into the boat when it was put over the side of the *Heron* the night of the storm. In the excitement, his presence had not been discovered, and the big rowboat had made it to shore. Old Jock knew that he had to get to the tower and he had started out. Everything had been all right, so he thought. No one had seen him, and he had raced along the cliffs. Suddenly, as he reached the cliffs near the tower, he had been grabbed from behind. He had cried out in surprise and then with pain as he grappled with two men.

"I did hear ye, then, Grandda!" cried Tammie. "Miss Cherry, we did hear Grandda that night."

"Yes, Tammie, I know now that we did."

"And I ran down from the tower," continued Tammie. "Some men caught me and they took me down the Old Mine shaft. But I kicked and bit and scratched and I got away."

"Tammie dear," said Meg, "do you mean to say that you found your way in the dark to the hidey-hole in Rogues' Cave?"

Tammie shook his head. "No, Miss Meg. One of the men was chasing me and he had a light. But I could dodge out of his way, even if he could run faster. He chased me almost as far as the cave, then I crouched down behind a pillar. He looked around, but he dinna find me, so he left. It wasn't far from the hidey-hole, so I went in there and hid."

"You mean to say, Tammie," Cherry said, "that you haven't had anything to eat since that night!"

Tammie smiled. "Of course not," he answered. "Grandma gave me some sandwiches and apples to put in my coat pocket."

"I wish somebody would tell me, a poor medical man," said Dr. Mac, "how Little Joe and his men found the vein of silver in the Old Mine."

"I'll explain it," said Sir Ian.

Everyone looked at him, rather surprised that he should know the answer.

"And Cherry knows," added Sir Ian.

"I do?" exclaimed Cherry.

Sir Ian nodded. "Of course ye found out about the real silver mine first and the salted mine second. But Little Joe, like most of the Balfourians, knew the story about how one George Barclay years ago was fooled by a grafter who salted our old abandoned mine. Now when Little Joe was working for me, he used to spend a lot of time fishing out in Rogues' Cave bay. He must have explored both the cave and the Old Mine from one end to the other. He discovered some of the salted stuff no doubt, then one day he discovered a rock that he knew was the real thing. And he went quietly to work."

"But I can't see—of course, I'm just a medical man—" said Dr. Mac, "how the vein of silver could have been missed during all the years that the Old Mine was in operation."

"I can answer that," said Lloyd. "You see, the Old Mine had veins of iron ore that ran north and south. When they were exhausted, the mine was abandoned. Yet just fifty feet away from one of the tunnels was this vein—this wonderfully rich vein—of native silver. The vein of silver begins in that alcove where we found Jock Cameron. It slopes gradually downward close to the tunnel in Rogues' Cave and becomes submarine. There's no telling how far out the vein runs beneath the ocean. Old Sir Ian, my grandfather, found some rocks of native silver in the cave walls without ever discovering the vein itself. That we know thanks to Cherry, who, with Tammie, found the journal and the pouch of silver in the tower room. Since my grandfather did not find the vein and surely had heard later of the cave's having been 'salted,' he probably decided that he'd found some of the 'salted' silver."

Higgins came in. "Luncheon is served," he announced.

Sir Ian offered his arm to Cherry. "Allow me to take you in, Cherry. For ye are the guest of honor. The Old Mine is going to have a new name. The Balfour silver mine will be officially named the Cherry Ames Silver Mine."

"Three cheers for Cherry Ames!" shouted Tammie.

"Yes, indeed, three cheers for Cherry," cried Meg and Lloyd, Old Jock, and Dr. Mac.

When they were all seated at the table, Cherry looked round at the friendly faces and her heart felt warm inside her.

"Thank you all," she said. "You have made me very happy. When I go back home, I shall take back with me wonderful memories of Balfour Island."

"What do you mean—when you go back home?" asked Meg. "Why, you have to stay ever so long. You have to be maid of honor at Douglas's and my wedding. Isn't that so, Dr. Douglas Mackenzie?"

"Absolutely," Dr. Mac agreed firmly.

"Ah, she'll make a fair maid of honor, won't she, Ian?" asked Old Jock. "And she'll bring us luck for sure with the siller mine."

"That she will, Jock," said Sir Ian, smiling warmly at his old friend.